THE TRUTH ABOUT ALICE

THE TRUTH ABOUT ALICE

JENNIFER MATHIEU

SQUARE
FISH

ROARING BROOK PRESS · NEW YORK

SQUARE FISH

An imprint of Macmillan Publishing Group, LLC
175 Fifth Avenue
New York, NY 10010
fiercereads.com

Square Fish books may be purchased for business or promotional use.
For information on bulk purchases, please contact the Macmillan Corporate
and Premium Sales Department at (800) 221-7945 x5442 or by e-mail
at specialmarkets@macmillan.com.

Library of Congress Cataloging-in-Publication Data

Mathieu, Jennifer.
    The truth about Alice / Jennifer Mathieu.
        pages cm
    Summary: "When ugly rumors and lies about Alice Franklin start after one
of the guys she allegedly slept with at a party dies in a car accident, questions
about truth arise in her small town"—Provided by publisher.
    ISBN 978-1-250-06302-1 (paperback) / ISBN 978-1-59643-910-8 (ebook)
    [1. Rumor—Fiction. 2. Truth—Fiction. 3. Bullying—Fiction.] I. Title.
    PZ7.M4274Tr 2014   [Fic]—dc23   2013044974

Originally published in the United States by Roaring Brook Press
First Square Fish Edition: 2015
Book designed by Elizabeth H. Clark
Square Fish logo designed by Filomena Tuosto

16 15 14 13 12 11 10 9 8 7

AR: 5.6 / LEXILE: 900L

For all the Alice Franklins

I, ELAINE O'DEA, AM GOING TO TELL YOU

two definite, absolute, indisputable truths.

1. Alice Franklin slept with two guys *in the very same night* in a bed IN MY HOUSE this past summer, just before the start of junior year. She slept with one and then, like five minutes later, she slept with the other one. Seriously. And everybody knows about it.

2. Two weeks ago—just after Homecoming—one of those guys, Brandon Fitzsimmons (who was crazy super popular and gorgeous and who yours truly messed around with more than once) died in a car accident. And it was all Alice's fault.

The other guy Alice slept with was this college guy, Tommy Cray, who used to go to Healy High. I'll get to Healy in a minute, and Brandon dying, too, but first, I should probably tell you about Alice.

It's weird, because *Alice Franklin* doesn't sound like a slutty name. It sounds like the name of a girl who takes really super good Chem notes or volunteers at the Healy Senior Center on Friday nights passing out punch and cookies or whatever it is they do at the Healy Senior Center on a Friday night. Speaking of old people, Alice sounds like a total grandma name. Like tissues-tucked-in-the-sleeves I-can't-find-my-purse what-time-is-*Jeopardy!*-on-again grandma. But that's totally not Alice Franklin. Hell no.

Because Alice Franklin is a slut.

She's not *overtly* slutty looking or whatever, but her look could go either way. She's a little taller than average but not freakishly tall, and I totally admit she has a really good figure. She never has to worry about her weight. Maybe her mom makes her count Weight Watchers points with her like mine does, but then again I don't think so, because Alice's mom doesn't seem to care that the entire town thinks her daughter is a total ho. I don't know if Alice's dad would care because Alice hasn't had a dad for as long as I've known her. Which is forever.

Alice has short hair that's cut sort of pixie-style, and she's one of those girls with naturally full lips. She always, always has raspberry-colored lipstick and lip liner on. Her face is standard pretty. She has multiple piercings in both ears, but she's not weird or punk or whatever; I guess she just likes a lot of earrings. In fact, she kind of dresses up for school. Or at least she did before all of this went down. She liked to wear pencil skirts and tight tops which showed off her boobs, and she'd always have on these open-toed sandals that showed off her raspberry toenails. Like even in February.

After it all happened, it's like she didn't care what she looked like. At first she came to school dressed all normal, but lately she's been showing up in jeans and a sweatshirt with the hood up lots of the time. She still wears the lipstick, though, which I find weird.

She hasn't ever been super crazy popular like me (I know that comes out conceited, but it's just the truth), but she's never been like that freak show Kurt Morelli who has an IQ of 540 and never talks to anyone except the teachers. If you're thinking of popularity as an apartment building, somebody like me is sitting on the roof of the penthouse, the band geeks are sleeping on the floor in the basement, and that freak show Kurt Morelli isn't living in the building at all. And I guess Alice Franklin has spent most of her life on some middle floor somewhere, but on the top of the middle.

So she was cool enough to come to my party.

You need to understand that this thing with Alice sleeping with two guys and Brandon dying in a car accident are *the* two biggest things to go down in Healy in a really super crazy long time. I don't mean just big with the kids who go to Healy High.

I mean big with like everyone. You know how there's this whole world that exists only to teenagers, and adults never know what's going on there? I think even the adults are aware of this phenomenon. Even they realize that they don't know what a certain word means or why a certain show is popular or like how they always get so excited to show you a YouTube video with a cat sneezing that you already saw twenty hundred years ago or whatever.

But Alice sleeping with two guys and then Brandon dying have become part of the whole world of Healy. Moms have talked about it with other moms at meetings of the Healy Boosters, they've asked their daughters about it, and they've looked at Alice's mom in the grocery store with a look that's always, "I feel so sorry for you, you terrible, terrible mother." (I know this because my mother has done all these things, including staring at Alice's mother in the dairy aisle while looking for some fat-free pudding she'd heard about at a Weight Watchers meeting. The pudding was only two points, so of course my mother was nuts for it.)

And this thing about Brandon dying is even crazier because he was Brandon Fitzsimmons, King of Healy, Texas. Quarterback and totally handsome and funny and everybody knew him. The dads have been talking about it at meetings of the Healy Boosters and in line at the Auto Zone, and they shake their heads and say what a damn shame it is that Brandon Fitzsimmons had to die in a car accident just a few weeks into football season. (I know this because my father has done all of

these things, including wondering out loud why that Alice Franklin Slut, as he put it, had to go and mess up Healy's best chance
at the 3A State Championship since he played for the Tigers
back in, like, 1925.)

Football is enormous in Healy, but Healy itself is not. It's
basically the kind of place that is just far enough away from the
city that it can't really be considered a suburb, but it's not big
enough to be considered much more than just a small town.
There are two grocery stores, three drugstores, and, like, five
billion churches located in strip malls. The movie theater shows
one movie at a time, so you never get a new one, and the big
thing to do on the weekends if you're under twenty is go get fast
food and beers and park in the Healy High parking lot and talk
shit about people or hope that someone's parents go out of town
so you can have a party. Most people either love it here and
never plan on leaving, or they hate it here and can't wait to go.

Healy isn't as bad as it sounds. I know it's totally lame that
the biggest store is a Walmart and we have to drive an hour and
ten minutes to go to a real mall, but still, I love it. I guess, yeah,
it's all I know, but I love walking into almost any store in town
and people know me and smile at me, and they ask me about
my mom and dad and they ask me if I'm on the varsity dance
squad this year (yes) and if I'm planning on being on the junior
prom committee (yes) and if I think Healy has a chance at state
(always). And the things I do seem to be the things that everyone else at Healy High wants to do. Like when my girlfriends
and I were freshmen and we started using toothpicks to write

5

letters on our nails with fingernail polish, so we could spell out ten-digit messages like I AM SO CUTE! and SCHOOL SUX! In about a week practically every other freshman girl at Healy High was copying us.

But back to Alice Franklin.

In the movies, high school parties are always these huge, crazy events with five hundred kids jammed into one house and naked people jumping from the roof into the pool, but in reality, high school parties are nothing like this. At least not in Healy. Healy parties basically consist of people sitting around the living room drinking, texting each other from across the room, watching television, and every once in a while someone goes into the kitchen to get another beer. Sometimes two people will go upstairs to one of the bedrooms and everyone makes a joke about it, and around midnight or 1 a.m. people pass out on the couch or go home.

Not so exciting sounding, I know, but I suppose what makes them exciting is the possibility that one of these nights, at one of these parties, something will happen.

And I guess that something did.

Kelsie

THE NIGHT OF ELAINE O'DEA'S PARTY, I WAS
throwing up and had a fever of 102.

So I didn't go.

This was truly an epic emergency in my eyes because despite
being almost a junior in high school, the old Kelsie from Flint
was not completely dead and buried inside of me yet. Back when I
lived in Michigan, I was a nerd. A nothing. A nobody. In Healy
I am *popular*, and this blows my mind, and I guess the night of
the party there was this part of me that was sure that if I missed
even one opportunity to remind everyone of my social standing,
I would be kicked back to the solitary cafeteria table of doom,
destined to live out the rest of my high school days completely
on my own. I would have to give up the fun that came with
being part of this super elite club where there was no secret

handshake or door knock, but there was still plenty to make it worthwhile.

I mean, to be totally honest, it's not like I'm on the very top rung of the social ladder like Elaine O'Dea and her crew, but if for whatever reason Elaine O'Dea and her friends are ever unable to perform their duties as the Most Popular Girls at Healy High, I am happy to be part of that Most Popular Girls Runners-Up group that is totally available to step in. And even as a runner-up I have privileges. Like . . . the feeling I get when I walk into the cafeteria and I know I can sit anywhere I want and people will *always* want to sit with me, and the fact that I *know* the teachers will already know my name on the first day of school without me having to tell them, and the fun in not worrying for even *one second* about whether or not I will have people to hang out with on the weekends. I *always* have people to hang out with on the weekends. Or anytime. Texting, talking, calling, drinking, kissing, laughing, dancing, drinking, texting, talking, and drinking. And I'm right in the middle of all of it.

I've seen the other side of things back in Flint, and I am here to tell you that being popular is awesome.

But I was so sick the night of Elaine's party, I didn't even pretend there was a chance I could show up. I just clutched the rim of the toilet bowl and cursed to myself as I thought about Elaine and Alice and Josh and Brandon and everybody sitting around together, and me not being a part of everything.

I hated not being a part of things. I hated missing things.

As it turns out, I did miss something. I missed The Thing that everyone would talk about all year long, and I knew I'd missed it the next morning as I ate dry toast and sipped ginger ale and listened to my best friend Alice Franklin on the other end of the phone.

"Tell me the truth, has anyone texted you about it?" Alice said, her voice low and serious. If it had been me, I would have been crying. But Alice wasn't crying. Not yet.

"I just got, like, one text about it." In reality I had gotten three texts, but I didn't see the point in telling this to Alice. The first text had been from this crazy sophomore who prides herself on spreading gossip, and it said:

Alice did Tommy Cray AND Brandon F. at Elaine's
party. OMG.

My stomach sort of gurgled a little when I read the text, and it wasn't from the stomach flu. It was mostly because of what it said about Alice, but it was also because it mentioned Tommy Cray, who I hadn't even realized was going to be at the party. I guess it was one last hurrah for him before going back to college for his sophomore year, but any mention of Tommy Cray and I'm forced to think about The Really Awful Stuff that happened to me last summer. No one knows about it. Not even Alice.

"Kelsie, it isn't true. You know it isn't true. I don't know why the hell Brandon is telling people this shit. Nothing happened!

We were hanging out at the party and he tried to mess around, and I was sort of buzzed and told him I didn't want to, and then I left. Nothing happened! You believe me, don't you?"

"Of course I believe you," I said.

And I did.

But I also didn't.

Honestly, I didn't know what to believe.

Which I guess should sort of tell you something about Alice Franklin. I mean, there was that time she lied to me about what she did with the lifeguard at Healy Pool North. And everyone still talks about what happened between her and Brandon and Elaine back in eighth grade. She had to know everyone was going to remember that. Maybe that was why I could sort of hear panic in her voice even if she was trying really hard to play it cool.

And to be honest, maybe I started to panic, too. I think right then I started to wonder if being Alice Franklin's best friend might spell trouble for me. I mean, if people didn't think what she'd done was a big deal, it would be okay. Probably. But what if it upped the slut factor so much that people started thinking I was a slut by association? I mean, it was one thing to be a girl who'd had sex. But it was something else entirely to be a girl who'd had sex with two guys in one night.

But I had to at least pretend to believe Alice. She'd been my first friend in Healy and my ticket into the world of social acceptance, and at first I wasn't sure how the party rumor would be received. It's true. If you haven't realized it, I'm aiming for truth here. Total honesty. And if the party rumor hadn't turned Alice into this kind of weird pariah from the first day of school on, it would have been easy to decide what to do. Even if the rumors did involve Tommy Cray, it would have been simple to choose to stay friends with her. I would have just gone along with what everybody wanted. But honestly, if what Alice did (or maybe didn't) do had been held up as some great achievement by everyone at Healy High, I would have still hung out with her. If everyone still liked her, I would have still liked her, too.

I know I sound like the worst person on Earth. I'm totally owning that.

It's like when we read *The Diary of Anne Frank* in seventh grade, and I had the sneaking suspicion that I would have been a Nazi back then because I wouldn't have had the guts to be anything else. Because I would have been too scared to not go along with the majority. Like, I would have been a passive sort of Nazi, but I still would have been a Nazi. I never said anything out loud, of course, but I remember reading that book in Ms. Peterson's class and everyone was all, "Oh, I would've helped Anne. I would have rebelled. I don't understand how people could have allowed this to happen, blah blah blah." I mean, I know that everyone wants to believe *they* would have been the brave one, and *they* would have been the one to hide Anne in their attic, and *they* would have killed Hitler with their own bare hands. But clearly if *everybody* thinks that way and in reality only a *few* people actually did it way back then, doesn't that just make me the honest one?

Anyway, the party was at the very end of the summer, and we'd only been back at school for a little while when Brandon died. The accident happened just a few weeks ago, right after Homecoming. And that was when stuff started getting really nuts because Brandon's best friend Josh Waverly, who had been in the car with Brandon when the accident happened, told Brandon's mom that the crash had been Alice's fault. Things were bad for Alice before the accident, but then it became like this whole other epic level of bad.

Alice called me crying about the car accident rumor, and I told her I was so sorry, and I was sure it wasn't true. When she called me after that I just didn't answer. She didn't call me all last week, and maybe she never will again. A few times she called and I answered and then acted like my mom wanted me to help make dinner or something. Once, back at the very beginning of the year before things got really bad and before Brandon died, she asked me to hang out with her and watch corny musicals at her house like we did back in ninth grade, and then when the weekend came I told her I was sick, but it was actually because Elaine O'Dea had invited me and some other girls over to her house. Like I'm going to turn down Elaine O'Dea to hang out with (allegedly) the biggest slut in the school?

The truth is, in the last few weeks, I've started "forgetting" to meet her at her locker before lunch and I've just gone straight to the cafeteria, and by the time she shows up, there's only one empty seat way at the end of the table in no-man's land. Sometimes no chair at all. I've just sort of shrugged my shoulders and done some halfhearted wave at her. Because I've been so chicken—because I *am* so chicken—that I didn't want Alice to be mad at me. How stupid is that? I wanted her to leave me alone, but I didn't want to deal with the uncomfortableness of having her upset with me for ignoring her. Totally hypocritical, I know.

We haven't had some blowup or some drama-filled fight or anything. Nothing like that. Just little by little, Alice Franklin was my best friend and then she was my friend and then she was sort of my friend and now I guess she isn't my friend at all.

The hard truth is I think I knew we weren't going to be friends anymore the day after Elaine's party when I read that text about her and Brandon and Tommy Cray. It sounds terrible and shallow and not at all like something the Kelsie Sanders I knew in Flint would have said, but I've spent too many years sitting alone in the cafeteria, and I just can't handle doing it again.

And I won't.

JOSH

I DON'T REMEMBER TOO MUCH ABOUT THE
accident. I woke up in the hospital not knowing what was going
on, and then my dad came in and told me what had happened
and that Brandon was dead. I remember feeling like I sort of left
my body. I'd heard about stuff like that on TV shows, and for a
second I thought maybe I was dying, too. Even though my dad
had already told me the doctors had said I was out of danger,
mostly because I'd been wearing my seat belt.

After I'd been awake for an hour or so, Officer Daniels of the
Healy Police came in to ask me some questions. I'd seen him
through the doorway of my hospital room, talking things over
with my parents. When he came in my mom followed, and she
sat down next to me on a green vinyl chair.

"You and Brandon had a few beers before you took off?"

Officer Daniels said real casually, thumbing through his little notepad and not looking at me. He didn't even sit down.

I didn't answer him right away. The room smelled like pee and bleach, and it made me kind of queasy.

"Son, we have your blood alcohol content and Brandon's, too," he said, "and both were above the legal limit. So there's no need to play coy." I guess I felt a little relieved when he told me that. So I said that yeah, me and Brandon had downed a couple of beers before Brandon's mom had asked us to head to Seller Brothers to get some diapers for his little sister.

Officer Daniels scratched his notepad with his pencil a couple of times.

"Any other reason Brandon might have been distracted?" he asked.

I wasn't expecting that follow-up question. I squeezed my eyes shut, trying to clear my mind. I remembered the screech of the brakes before we ran off the road. I remembered how I'd bit down hard on my tongue when we crashed, and my mouth had filled up with blood. Like it was full of nickels and dimes.

I guess a while passed because my mom spoke up. "Josh? Is there anything else Officer Daniels needs to know about what happened?"

I stared at the chew marks on Officer Daniels's pencil. It looked like a rat had been gnawing on it. I tried not to think about the throbbing pain in my shoulder. I tried not to think about any-thing, actually.

"Well, Brandon was sort of fooling around with his phone," I said finally. "You know, like messing with it?"

Officer Daniels shook his head. "Too common these days," he announced to my mother, like I wasn't even there. He wrote down a few more things in his notepad, told me that he had everything he needed, and said he hoped I'd get better real fast.

"By the way," he said just before he turned around to leave, "great win at Homecoming, son."

"Thank you, sir," I said.

My mom and I just sat there for a little while in silence. Then she came over and kissed me on the forehead. She sniffed a little like maybe she was trying not to cry.

It's been almost a month since the accident and Brandon dying, and my body still isn't totally back to normal, but the doctor says I could probably be back on the football field with enough time to make the last few games of the season.

That's what he told me anyway, like that was what I was supposed to be the most concerned about. When I could play football again. Not my best friend dying or anything.

My mom and dad and younger brother keep looking at me like they think I'm going to disappear or something if they stop staring at me. Like maybe I was supposed to die in that accident or something, and it's just luck that I didn't, so they'd better keep looking just to be safe. Sometimes my mom cries when she looks at me. It's real uncomfortable.

Even with my broken collarbone and my sore muscles, I went to the funeral, of course. The funeral was crazy packed. I mean, even people who showed up on time had to stand in the back, and there were some people in the lobby area of the church just trying to hear even though they couldn't see. Even the mayor of Healy was there. Brandon's mom and dad and all his brothers and sisters were up front, and his mom was just sobbing all hysterical, which made all the moms and the girls sob even harder. The whole team and Coach Hendricks were up behind the family, and Coach Hendricks just kept shaking his head the whole time.

I think Alice is the only student at Healy High who didn't come to the funeral. Even Kurt Morelli was there with his grandma. I guess it makes sense since he lived next door to Brandon ever since we were all in kindergarten.

At the service, the pastor said all this stuff about Jesus and making sense of bad stuff, but I didn't really listen. I rubbed my hands on my knees, wiping the sweat off. I couldn't stop thinking about me being wide receiver and Brandon being the quarterback and how we'd practice together, just the two of us; it was like we never even had to talk to each other. We just always knew where the other guy was going to run, where the other guy was going to throw. I thought about how Brandon would throw these perfect spirals and they would just fall into my hands so easy. Swish, thump. Swish, thump. Swish, thump. We could do it over and over and over again.

We talked without talking.

I think about Brandon and I think about the funeral and I think about the hospital, and I think about that day a few days after they'd buried Brandon. The day his mom came over to our house to see me. My mom was still making me spend most of my days resting on the couch in the den, like she was afraid to let me out of her sight.

"God, Josh, if only I'd known Brandon had been drinking, I wouldn't have ever asked him to go to the store," Mrs. Fitzsimmons said. "But honey, I'm not an idiot. Brandon wasn't a stranger to a couple of beers. The police said it was the drinking that probably caused the accident, but Officer Daniels said you mentioned something about Brandon's phone? What can you tell me, sweetheart? I feel like there's something you aren't saying. Please, Josh. I just want to know everything that happened that day."

The television was on mute. I stared at ESPN for a minute. Mrs. Fitzsimmons was just sitting there on the edge of my dad's old recliner. My mom had given her a glass of sweet tea that she held in her lap but she didn't drink it. She just sort of clutched it with her hands.

"Well, I mean . . ." I started. My heart was pounding real hard.

"I know you don't want to make trouble, but I feel like there's got to be another explanation than he just had a few beers," Mrs. Fitzsimmons said. She put the glass down on the coffee table and reached out for my hands. Her hands were cold and clammy. Maybe from holding the sweet tea. Maybe just because they were. And I thought about all the times I'd been over to Brandon's house since I'd been a kid. The millions of times. And how Mrs. Fitzsimmons was always so nice to me and everything, almost like another mom.

And I felt my mouth moving and words just coming out, and all of a sudden I was telling her about Alice's texts.

"Alice Franklin?" Mrs. Fitzsimmons asked, her forehead wrinkling up.

I nodded. I mean, it was kind of embarrassing because she was Brandon's mom, but I'm sure even Mrs. Fitzsimmons had heard the rumors about Alice and Brandon and what had happened at Elaine's party at the end of the summer. Everyone had been talking about Alice since then. Even the grown-ups.

So I told her how when we'd been on the road, Alice had been sending Brandon all these texts and she wouldn't stop.

"Texts? What do you mean texts?" Mrs. Fitzsimmons said. "What would she be texting him about?" I looked at the television screen and I looked at the glass of sweet tea on the coffee table. But I couldn't look at Mrs. Fitzsimmons.

"Uh, I'm sorry, but this is sort of awkward," I said.

"No, it's okay, Josh. The texts, were they, like, harassing?"

"They were, like, uh, sexual stuff," I said. "Like stuff about that party and, uh, stuff she wanted to do to Brandon or whatever."

"How many times did she text him while he was trying to drive?" Mrs. Fitzsimmons asked.

"Lots. I mean, I lost count. They were popping up every second or so."

Mrs. Fitzsimmons nodded and I guess you could say she looked upset, but her face relaxed a little, like maybe there was a part of her that was also relieved. She finally took a sip of her tea.

"So you could say she was distracting him with her texts?" Mrs. Fitzsimmons asked.

"Yeah," I answered. "You could say he was distracted."

"Thank you, Josh. Thank you for telling me that. I know it wasn't easy."

I nodded, and I was glad when she switched the topic to Brandon's funeral and how touched she was that so many people came out for it and how happy Brandon would have been about that. We sat there for a little bit longer, just talking about Brandon and how much we both missed him, and Mrs. Fitzsimmons had to dab at her eyes a little with her napkin and stop every so often so she didn't start crying really hard. When she decided to leave, she hugged me, but not too tight on account of my shoulder.

"Josh, sweetie, I just want you to know you're welcome at our house anytime," she said. "Anytime, honey. I don't want to lose touch with you. I hope you know that."

I nodded again, wishing she would just go home. I felt bad about feeling that way, but I just wanted to be by myself.

On her way out, she stopped in the kitchen to talk to my mom, and I could catch little bits and pieces of what they were saying over all of the yelling on ESPN. Now I love my mom and everything, but she doesn't exactly have the best habit of keeping stuff to herself. And in a town like Healy, information like the kind I'd just shared with Mrs. Fitzsimmons travels pretty fast. I guess my mom must have told someone else's mom, and that mom told another mom, and maybe that mom told her kid. You get the idea. Anyway, the bottom line is that by the time I started back at school, Alice Franklin wasn't just that slut who'd slept with Tommy Cray and Brandon Fitzsimmons at some party.

She was the slut who got Brandon Fitzsimmons killed.

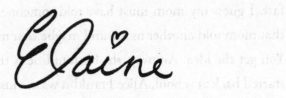

Elaine

BRANDON AND I WERE NEVER BOYFRIEND AND
girlfriend. Like official, we-celebrate-monthly-anniversaries,
I-have-a-framed-picture-of-him-in-my-bedroom kind of boyfriend. I mean, I've *had* boyfriends like that. When I was younger,
they were usually upperclassmen, and they were always popular. I started dating guys when I was in seventh grade. Other girls
couldn't go out that young, but my mom was okay with it. I
mean, my dad wasn't. But my mom sort of talked him into it as
long as the guy came over to our house first and shook his hand
and blah blah blah.

But the thing is, as I've grown up, there've just been fewer
and fewer available guys around here who are older than me and
who are my type. Which left Brandon. I know this is going to
sound totally conceited, but, like, as the most popular girl and
guy in our class, we naturally ended up together sometimes.

And by that I mean we went to sophomore Homecoming together and we made out at parties pretty regularly and when I
was bored or he was bored, we would go over to each other's
houses and yes, okay, fine, I did sleep with him a few times last
year. (Oh my God, if my dad knew he would just have a stroke
and die. Even if Brandon was the best quarterback Healy
ever had.)

Anyway, I'm not saying he was like my property or whatever,
but there was this unspoken thing that everyone knew, which
was that Brandon Fitzsimmons and I were sort of with each
other when we weren't busy figuring out who else we could be
with. It was, um, the natural order of things. We were on again,
off again, on again, off again, wash, rinse, repeat.

Until that Sunday when he got in his truck with Josh Waverly
and they headed to Seller Brothers.

The news that Brandon died spread faster than the news about
Alice at my party. I heard about it from Maggie, one of my best
friends, who heard about it almost right away because her father
is a Healy police officer.

She called me the afternoon that it happened, totally sobbing—
she couldn't even breathe.

"Elaine, I'm so so so totally sorry, but Brandon Fitzsimmons
is dead," she said.

I just sat there on my bed, holding my phone, and I cried for
him. And for me. For us.

I thought about how gorgeous he was. How you could stare
at him all day long, even when he was being kind of an asshole,

and you could just appreciate his face for what it was. Which was perfect.

And I thought about junior high, when he used to snap my bra strap and wink at me in the cafeteria and squeeze my butt in the hall. It was the first time I'd started to realize I was cute to boys, even if my mom was already making me go to Weight Watchers and I was already worried that my butt was kind of big.

And I thought about that weird, totally embarrassing thing that happened between us the night of my infamous party—him pinning me down on my bed, his eyes looking at nothing, his breath stinking of beer.

And I thought about him doing it with Alice Franklin later on at that very same party in my guest bedroom, the two of them laughing about me before Tommy Cray took his turn.

Alice.

I knew I could never trust that girl.

On the day I found out about Brandon, I also thought about the eighth grade dance—when Brandon and I were absolutely and totally *on again*, but later Alice swore to me up and down she didn't know, she thought nothing was going on between us, and she hadn't really wanted to kiss Brandon that much to begin with even though she had. I mean, okay, I get that it was eighth grade and Brandon's voice had barely changed and none of us could even drive yet or whatever, but still. It just goes to show you what Alice Franklin is like. At the dance—which I had arrived at *with Brandon*, I will have you know—Alice ended up making out with him in the coat closet. A few of my girlfriends found them and ran and told me, and after walking in on them and screaming at them both, I ended up spending half the dance in the bathroom crying and asking everyone if my mascara was running.

Brandon apologized a bajillion times, and then we were off again until we were on again. Again. But I never forgot what Alice Franklin did to me, and neither did anyone else. Which makes it very easy to believe the rumor about her at my party. It's just the kind of thing a girl like Alice would do.

And it makes it even easier to believe the rumor about her and the car accident and those texts.

She's just a skank.

I honestly don't see how Alice Franklin is going to recover from all this. I really don't think she will. After the party she tried so hard to act like nothing ever happened, even coming up and trying to sit with us and everything in the cafeteria. It was kind of pathetic. Even her best friend, Kelsie, doesn't want anything to do with her anymore, and that was before Brandon died. But since the accident . . . well, I guess it's not possible since not going to school is against the law, but it would've almost been better for Alice Franklin if she never even came back to Healy High.

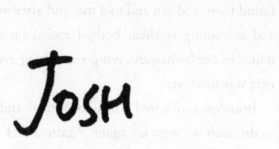

JOSH

THE AFTERNOON OF ELAINE O'DEA'S PARTY,
Brandon Fitzsimmons and I were talking about tits.

The deal was, you could open Brandon's bedroom window
and get out onto the roof of the first floor of his house. Lots of
times we would climb out there and drink beers and talk about
Coach Hendricks's plays or what teacher was making us crazy
or what girls in Healy High had the best tits. That's what we
were talking about the afternoon of Elaine's party.

"I'm thinking about Elaine right now," Brandon said, reaching up with both hands like he was giving the clouds in the sky
a feel. "She's got a nice set."

"You're sick," I said, opening up my Natty Light. It was
Brandon's dad's beer of choice and so it was our beer of choice,
too.

It was usually hot as hell up there, even with the beers. We didn't go out there much during the summer, but the day of Elaine's party it was kind of overcast, so it wasn't too bad. And anyway, after a couple of Natty Lights we didn't mind the sun. Our muscles were aching after Two-A-Days all week, and nothing would help us relax more than the roof and some cold beer. Brandon's parents were home, and they probably knew we were drinking beer. But they didn't care. Brandon could get away with anything.

"Look at that dude," Brandon drawled, motioning to Kurt Morelli. I looked down at the yard to the right. Kurt was hunched over an old lawnmower from maybe 1984 or something. I didn't see how he could even really push it he was so small and skinny. He kept stopping now and then to wipe the sweat off his face. He was a puny guy, and I felt sorry for him just watching him.

"Glad I'm not mowing my grandma's lawn," I said, enjoying the Natty Light buzz that was settling on me.

"Mark my words, man," Brandon said, "that dude is never going to get any pussy. Ever."

"Not like you, King of All Pussy," I said, wishing we had more beer.

"It's true," Brandon said.

And it was true.

Brandon was like a God in Healy, and I guess I was like God's best friend. He was God of the football team and God of the school and God of the town. Everywhere he went, people knew him. Old people knew him, little kids in grade school knew him, fucking Mexicans who moved here five seconds ago and didn't even know English knew him. Everybody knew Brandon Fitzsimmons.

Brandon got more action than any other guy I knew. He'd even slept with Ms. Sanchez, this chick who teaches Spanish part-time at Healy High. She's like twenty-four with a pretty great body, and Brandon said he needed help with Spanish and he just showed up at her house, and according to Brandon they did it on the kitchen table while her husband was at work.

I've only done it once. The summer before sophomore year when I was fifteen. It was at the beach and it was this girl named Tessa, and her family was staying at the beach house next to my family's beach house, and we did it one night down on the sand after we'd gone for a walk. I found us this sort of private hiding spot near some rocks and we did it. Tessa brought the condoms. All I could think about when it was over was at least I could finally say I did it. Tessa and me still text sometimes, but this summer our families didn't go down to the beach at the same time.

Brandon was always getting after me to get with someone else. I'm not saying this to sound like a dick or anything, but I could probably get action with lots of girls in our class in about five seconds if I wanted to. But for some reason a lot of the girls in our class annoy the piss out of me. They always act like everything is some stupid huge crisis or drama or whatever, and they always want to talk about everything for five hundred years. They remind me of grackles sitting around on a telephone wire getting ready to swoop at some worm.

It was like Brandon was reading my mind the afternoon of Elaine's party, because after we talked about Kurt Morelli, he said, "Speaking of pussy, you should try to get some action tonight with Maggie Daniels. Her panties get wet every single time you walk by her locker."

"Jesus, man," I said, trying to drag out the last of my last Natty Light.

"Whatever, dude, it's true."

Then, I guess just so I could be saying something, just so I could be getting the attention off of me, I said, "What about you and Alice Franklin? Just the other day I saw you checking her out when we were all hanging out in the parking lot."

I don't know why I picked Alice since Brandon checked out just about every girl he ever saw in the parking lot and everywhere else. I guess she was just sort of floating around in my head. I mean, Alice and me had known each other since before we could even be aware that we knew each other. Me and her were even in the same day care at the Methodist church near my house when we were little.

Brandon said, "Alice Franklin? Hell. I haven't messed around with her since that middle school dance when Elaine lost her shit."

"You've never done it with Alice?" I asked. I guess that surprised me because Alice was definitely a chick who had done it. She started having boyfriends in fifth grade. She kind of had a reputation for being a little crazy. Like how in eighth grade she made out with Brandon at the graduation dance even though he showed up with Elaine. Plus there was that rumor about her and that lifeguard at Healy Pool North.

"No, I've never done it with Alice, but now you've gone and put an idea in my head," Brandon said. He peered over at Kurt Morelli who had stopped mowing the lawn and had his hands on his hips and was just staring out at nothing.

"Hey, Kurt, my man. Wanna come up and have a beer?" I don't know why Brandon said this seeing as we had no beers left and Kurt Morelli is a pretty weird dude, but I think Brandon was pretty wasted by then.

"No libations, thank you, sir," Kurt yelled up, waving his right hand at us like a salute, and Brandon and me just looked at each other like what the hell is this guy talking about.

So after that me and Brandon peeled ourselves off the roof and we went inside, and I had to steady myself for a little while before I felt sober enough to drive home. I lay back on Brandon's twin bed with the football bedspread he'd had since he was ten.

"Do? You? Want? To? Sleep? With? Me?" Brandon said out loud as he texted Elaine about the beer for the party, like making it look like he was texting Elaine about doing it with him. But he was just joking about Elaine. Elaine was sort of old news to Brandon. I knew now he was really thinking about Alice Franklin because he kept bringing her up.

"I've never done it with a girl with real short hair before like that," Brandon said. "I hope doing it with Alice wouldn't be like doing it with a dude. Because that would be gross. That would be gay."

30

Man, I felt hot and tired that day. At that moment I didn't even know if I wanted to go to the party. The Natty Light made me feel like going to sleep, but even as I thought that, I knew I would be going to the party to drink even more Natty Lights. There wasn't anything else to do.

"Maybe you *are* gay," I said. "You've seen me naked two hundred times."

"Dude, if you think I'm looking at you in those showers, you are one sick bastard," Brandon said.

I rolled over onto my stomach and sank my face into the football bedspread. It smelled like sweat and Tide. Brandon was saying something else about Alice Franklin's tits.

Sometimes I wonder if I hadn't put the idea of her into Brandon's head, if everything that happened wouldn't have happened. Because sometimes when Brandon got an idea into his head, it was like trying to sack him when he was about to throw a touchdown pass. What I mean is, it was impossible.

But that afternoon in Brandon's bedroom, lying facedown with my head sort of spinning, I didn't know that one day I would wonder what if. All I knew that afternoon was that I was drunk and I was Brandon Fitzsimmons's best friend and we were some of the best football players Healy had ever seen, and that night me and him were going to go to Elaine O'Dea's party.

Kurt

TO STATE THE BLATANTLY OBVIOUS, I WASN'T
invited to Elaine O'Dea's party.

To tell you the truth, I didn't even know there was a party at
Elaine O'Dea's, although I've always been aware that there are
parties and football games and other social events going on around
me. I've just never been invited to them, and even if I were to be
invited, I wouldn't attend. I see no need in taking part in forced
adolescent social rituals that would do nothing but stir up emotions of dread for all involved. I would dread having to interact
at such an event, and I know they would dread to see me show
up at the door.

In an effort to be completely fair, I suppose it's not techni-
cally true that I've never been invited. In elementary school,
I was invited. That was back when all of us were students at
Jefferson Elementary, and our quirks and strange rough edges

hadn't fully formed yet. We were just kids, and we all got along to a certain degree. What were parties back then anyway other than running around in the backyard and eating hot dogs off the grill? Besides, I think Brandon Fitzsimmons's parents and Elaine O'Dea's parents and all the other parents felt sorry for me. I was the orphan from Chicago.

Yes, it's true. It sounds Charles Dickensesque, but I'm an honest-to-God orphan and have been since the age of five. My parents were driving the Dan Ryan Expressway in a bad storm one Saturday evening, and the next day I was an orphan, shipped off to Healy to live with my dad's mom.

I have vague memories of my parents and Chicago. I remember I had plastic cereal bowls in every color of the rainbow, and I remember I liked to curl into my dad's armpit to watch PBS children's programming, and I remember when I hugged my mom she smelled of soap.

But then came Healy and the sad cluckety clucks from my grandmother's friends whenever we ran into them at the Kroger and the licensed clinical social worker who was always asking me to draw my feelings with crayons. Accelerate through time and I'm a junior in high school, and it's strange to think I ever lived anywhere else but here, with its oppressive summer heat and small town drama.

I don't exactly fit into the milieu that is Healy life. Why not? First, I've been told I'm sort of a genius. I even take online classes through the university nearby because some of the high school coursework isn't challenging enough for me. I'll admit to trying to read in the shower and using my free time to think about black holes folding in on themselves, but honestly, it's not like I *tried* to be a genius. I'm not even sure I am a genius, despite what the college counselor tells me. Maybe I'm just a genius by Healy standards.

Secondly, I do not play sports nor do I have an interest in sports at all.

Lastly, unlike my fellow citizens, I have the ability to recognize that Healy is simply an extremely small place in the middle of a very large place called the United States, and that the United States is itself also just a small place in the middle of an even larger place called the world, and that makes much of what is discussed in and around Healy inconsequential in the grand scheme of things.

So why don't I mind living here? First, everyone leaves me alone. Which is to say they ignore me. Which is not as bad as it sounds. To be honest, it's really rather nice to be afforded such freedom of time and of space to read, to think and study, and to be left in peace. When I sit by myself in the cafeteria rereading *The Hobbit* for the thirteenth time just because I want to, I don't look out onto the sea of faces and wish I wasn't alone. I simply acknowledge the sea exists and go back to *The Hobbit*. It isn't difficult for me.

Secondly, I haven't minded living in Healy because my grandmother is a loving and caring woman who has raised me with affection and compassion.

Lastly, Alice Franklin lives here.

Alice Franklin with the raspberry lips and the bad reputation and the faraway eyes. Alice Franklin with the short hair not like any other girl's and the gloriously loud laugh and the body that curves like an alpha wave. Alice Alice Alice Alice Franklin.

Oh, yes, I am a genius, but I am still a man. A man who lives in Healy. And Alice Franklin lives in Healy, which makes Healy worth living in.

Before Elaine O'Dea's party, I watched Alice Franklin from a very distant vantage point. I made mental notes. Not because I thought I would ever be able to achieve any sort of romantic re-lationship with her, but because taking note of the things she said and did made me feel like I knew her better, and this pro-vided me with more fodder for my daydreams of walking with Alice Franklin, of kissing Alice Franklin, of holding Alice Frank-lin's alpha waves close to my body.

Things I Noticed About Alice Franklin
Before Elaine O'Dea's Party

• Once when she was walking down the Foreign Lan-
    guage hall and a very skinny freshman boy dropped
    all of his books and some senior kicked them, Alice
    Franklin stopped and knelt down in her lime-colored
    pencil skirt and scooped them up in her arms and
    handed them to this boy and smiled at him. I remem-
    ber catching a glimpse of her knees as she knelt down.
    They were like two peach-flavored candies. She has
    tremendous knees.

- She doodled constantly in class. Flowers, apple pies, lizards, clocks, cats. Every margin of every notebook was covered. But she could doodle and still listen because sometimes she would be in the middle of a doodle of, say, a fish swimming in a stream, and she would stretch out her hand and ask a question.

- At lunch, she always ate the same thing every single day: tuna salad sandwich, pretzels, apple, lemonade.

- On the first day of tenth grade in Ms. Galanter's English class, when we had to make a list of our favorite things, I managed to glimpse and memorize the following: *favorite book*—The Outsiders, *favorite smell*—*fresh-cut grass, favorite sound*—*the French language, favorite day of the week*—*Saturday, favorite band*—*The Beatles.*

- Also during tenth grade I found her in the library after school trying to finish up homework for Geometry. She was leaning over her notebook and chewing the end of her pencil and writing and erasing and writing and erasing. I walked by and somewhere deep inside of my soul I found the temerity to ask her if she needed help. She said, "Well, do you have a sec?" I sat next to her. She smelled of vanilla. Her perfect cleavage was peeking out of a pink top. I had to struggle to explain the problem and ended up just doing it for her. When I was done, she said, "Thanks, Kurt." All the way home that afternoon I was smiling to myself because Alice Franklin called me by my name. Admittedly, there are only 150 people in our class, so everyone knows everyone else's name. But still, it was nice to hear my name uttered by her voice.

Even a recluse like me learned of the events that allegedly occurred at Elaine O'Dea's party, and even a recluse like me could have seen the slow shift in Alice Franklin's behavior and in the behavior of those she was normally surrounded by. The girls she sat with in the cafeteria have drifted away, one by one. There's quite an enormous difference between a person like me, who enjoys eating alone, and a person like Alice Franklin, who has had isolation placed upon her as a mark of shame. Lately, Alice Franklin doesn't even eat in the cafeteria.

Then Brandon Fitzsimmons died, not that long ago, and people have been claiming that Alice caused the accident by sending him inappropriate texts. It seems Alice has become magnetic for all sorts of negative attention. She's started coming to school dressed in a bulky sweatshirt. You can't see her perfect cleavage anymore. She's taken to wearing the hood up, even in the hallways. It's like she wants to disappear.

Yesterday, after the final bell, I was walking past the football stadium bleachers behind the school, and I saw Alice sitting there. Her face looked tearstained.

At that moment, it seemed like the opportunity I had been looking for. To talk to her. To tell her what I know. Because— and this was shocking—I know something about Alice. I know a fact, a truth—that might perhaps bring her relief but at the same time might perhaps only bring her more pain. I formed the words in my mouth, rolling my tongue over them, attempting multiple times to push them out through my lips. How idiotic I must have seemed just standing there, looking at her, saying nothing. Practicing words.

Finally, Alice noticed me.

"What the hell do you want?" she snapped. This time, she didn't call me Kurt.

"I . . ." I said, opening and closing my mouth. How desperately I wanted to tell her what I knew. How much I wanted to share the information I had that no one else at Healy High had a claim on but me.

"Seriously, what the hell?" she said, standing up and shoving her hands into the pockets of her hooded sweatshirt. She stomped off down the bleachers. "I'm not a sideshow attraction."

And she wasn't. Not to me.

She was the main attraction.

But I had no way to tell her that.

Kelsie

WE MOVED HERE FROM MICHIGAN BECAUSE my dad got a job working for his uncle as an electrician. Also, Jesus wanted us to come here. At least according to my mother, who is personal, best friends with Jesus Christ. Jesus has to okay everything with my mother before she does it. I guess he even okayed The Really Awful Stuff that happened to me last summer. But I don't know, because my mom and I have never talked about it since.

Anyway, before we left Flint to come here, I made a promise to myself. When I got to Healy, I wasn't going to sit by myself in the cafeteria reading a book and I wasn't going to sit in the front row in class answering all the questions just because I could. I was going to learn how to wear eyeliner and I was going to start figuring out what colors looked right with other colors and I was going to force my mother to let me start shaving my legs even if

Jesus said I shouldn't. I wasn't going to spend my weekends making shoebox dioramas by myself for fun and I was going to start talking to people who weren't my parents and I wasn't going to be the same lame Kelsie Sanders that I'd been all of my fourteen-year-old life.

I spent my last summer in Flint working so hard. Just like I'd once worked on my shoebox dioramas, I spent those weeks reading the magazines and watching the television shows that all the girls in my class talked about, trying to get as much information as I could about the right way to behave. I babysat for snotty Jerry Baker next door and saved up all my money for the right clothes and the right makeup, and when my mom told me Christian girls don't wear skinny jeans, I did it anyway.

"You're new, right?" Alice Franklin said to me that first day of ninth grade as I sat in the back row of Mrs. Henesey's homeroom.

"Yeah," I said, eyeing her raspberry lipstick and trying really hard not to look impressed. My mother might not have noticed my shaved legs, but she sure wasn't going to let me out of the house with raspberry lipstick on.

"Well, we're all new to high school, right?" she said, shrugging her shoulders. "Even if most of us have lived here for a bajillion years." She said *bajillion* like the word tasted like rotten eggs.

"Yeah," I answered, already picturing myself alone in the cafeteria since I could only come up with one-word answers.

"See that boy over there?" Alice said suddenly, pointing to a boy with short blond hair and a Texas Longhorns T-shirt on.

"Yeah?"

"Stay away from him. His name is Kyle Walker. We went out in middle school, and he's a *total* asshole."

Back then I never swore, not even privately in my head, and I know I started blushing.

Just then a pretty cute guy sitting next to us turned and asked Alice if she was free that weekend and wanted to hang out. And just at the moment when I knew I would never be cool enough for this girl, Alice said in her most bored voice possible, "Um, I'm free every weekend. It's in the constitution."

Before I could tell myself to *shut up, stupid!* I exclaimed, "Oh my God, do you know *Grease 2*? That's a line from *Grease 2*!"

That's how we became friends. We both liked to watch really stupid musicals like *Xanadu* and *Can't Stop the Music* and even *Paint Your Wagon*, and we both liked to eat frosting straight from the can, and we both thought Elaine O'Dea acted way cuter than she actually was. When Alice came over to my house for the first time, she didn't seem to be weirded out by the Smile! Jesus Loves You! pencils in the kitchen by the to-do list or the Bible Stories Bingo game on the coffee table. She was just nice about it, and during our third sleepover after we'd watched *Sgt. Pepper's Lonely Hearts Club Band* and we were buried in our sleeping bags and it was totally dark and the only sound was the air conditioner cycling on and off—when I chose that second to tell Alice Franklin that back in Flint I'd never had anyone over for a sleepover—Alice didn't laugh.

"I'm glad you had me over," she said. "I'm glad we're friends."

Even though I know I did what I had to do, and even though lately Alice has completely disappeared from my life and into her big bulky sweatshirt and wherever it is she goes to eat lunch . . . even though I don't regret what I did and I would do it again, it's that memory that hurts the most when I think about how I dumped Alice.

So she was my best friend for over two years. So how come I can't believe her? I mean, isn't that what a best friend does?

Well, partly it's because I'm too afraid I'll become some sort of nobody again if I do. I'll never be popular again. Like I've said, I'm owning that.

And partly it's because one of the guys she (may have) slept with at Elaine's party was Tommy Cray.

And partly it's because of last summer—the summer of The Really Awful Stuff—and because of something Alice did when she worked the snack bar at Healy Pool North.

Alice always made her own money. She babysat, walked dogs, anything. Once she even cleaned Mrs. Montgomery's house for a month while Mrs. Montgomery was recovering from back surgery. Alice always has to have her own money for clothes or magazines or makeup or whatever because her mother doesn't give her anything. Alice's mom is always complaining there isn't enough to go around with her being a single mom and all, but it doesn't seem to stop her from going out almost every night and leaving Alice to sort of fend for herself.

So the pool was like her first real job. One where she got a check she had to take to the bank instead of just a wad of rolled-up bills.

One of the perks of Alice's pool job was the free snacks Alice would sneak me. She didn't take total advantage or anything, but there'd be a Popsicle here or a candy bar there. I would sit on a stool outside the snack bar in the blue-and-white-striped bikini Alice had helped me pick out, and we would gossip and watch the boys swim, and I would help Alice make change when she got confused with the math.

The best perk, however, was the two high school seniors who worked there as lifeguards. Tommy Cray and Mark Lopez. They had just graduated from Healy High, and they were both so gorgeous. So totally gorgeous. The boys in our class still seemed like boys, but Tommy and Mark were men. At least that's what Alice was always saying.

"Why waste our time with boys when there are men right here at Healy Pool North?" she would say, admiring Mark's muscles or Tommy's grin.

I figured if any of my friends knew about men, it was Alice. She wasn't a virgin at that point and I still was. She'd lost her virginity freshman year to this junior named Tucker Bowles and then they'd broken up two months later, and this made Alice the expert in my eyes when it came to stuff like sex and boys. Or men.

I thought Tommy was gorgeous and had spent most of the summer secretly staring at him whenever I hung out at the pool, but I thought Tommy and Mark both sort of had crushes on Alice. I just didn't think either boy was interested in me. My problem basically was (and is) that I don't know how to relax around guys. I can't make that easy small talk with boys that some girls can. Girls like Elaine O'Dea and Maggie Daniels can do that weird, amazing thing where it looks like they're making fun of a boy on the surface, but somehow the boy always takes it as one big compliment.

Alice used to be good at that, too.

One night toward the end of that summer before tenth grade, Alice called me after the pool had closed and asked if I wanted to come down for a party. I told my mom I was going to go to Alice's to sleep over, but I had to convince her to let me go because she wasn't crazy about Alice (because Alice didn't have a personal relationship with Jesus Christ) and also because we had to go to the 8:00 a.m. service the next morning. (When I whined, she told me, "As for me and my house, Kelsie, I will serve the Lord.")

I don't know what I was thinking would be going on, but when I hopped off my ten speed and walked into the guard house, I found Alice and Tommy and Mark. That was the party. They had some beers, and they smelled of bleach from bleaching out the bathrooms. Even though I'd been hanging out at the pool most of the summer, I still wasn't as tan as the three of them. I remember Tommy had little pockets on his shoulders that were peeling, and the skin underneath was as pink as a brand-new eraser.

Alice was sort of drunk, I could tell, and she was sort of hanging on to Mark, cutting into his side with her elbow and laughing with him at some private joke.

"Let's swim," Tommy said. I think he sensed Alice and Mark wanted to be by themselves. I was glad I'd worn my bikini underneath my clothes.

The pool felt so different at night without the shrieks of middle school kids screaming Marco! Polo! or the tweets of the lifeguard whistle. After a beer, I dove in without making a splash and sank down to the bottom, letting my fingertips slide over the slippery black lane line markers. I broke through the water and dove down again immediately, wanting to stay there forever, enjoying the feeling of being slightly buzzed and underwater. Anyway, if I got out, I would have to talk to the heart-stopping Tommy. That seemed basically impossible.

"Where's Alice?" I asked, when I'd finally resurfaced. Tommy was sitting on the edge of the pool, his feet dangling in the water. He was sipping on a beer. He arched his eyebrows. He was gorgeous. Even now, after everything, I can still admit that.

"Where do you think?" he said, like I was slow.

I ducked back down under the water, wondering how long I should stay there or what I should say when I came back up. I loved Alice when we were alone together, eating ice cream or raw cookie dough or painting our toenails green or telling stupid jokes, but sometimes I felt left out whenever Alice was around a boy she liked.

Like I wasn't sure where I fit in.

And like I knew I'd never get a boy to like me in the same way.

When I resurfaced, I heard someone saying, "Hey, Kelsie, are you ready to go home?"

It was Alice, coming out of the girls' locker room, followed by Mark Lopez. Mark's face was a little red. Tommy gave him a look, and the two of them laughed. Alice tucked her fingers under the bottom of her wet green bikini and tugged on it, like she was straightening it back out. When she let go, it made a smacking sound on her rear end. Her body was perfect, and that wasn't the first time I'd noticed that fact with a lot of envy inside.

"Something happened with Mark, right?" I asked that night, the two of us alone in the dark of her bedroom, sharing her double bed. We'd been too tired to shower, and the sheets and the air and everything smelled of chlorine. I'd gathered up the courage to ask Alice that question because I knew I was going to be jealous of the answer. It was like I didn't want to hear it, but I couldn't help myself.

But Alice just laughed that loud honking Alice laugh.

"Oh my God, what?" she said, rolling over onto her stomach and turning her face away from me. "He's leaving in a week for college. We're just friends."

I remember the way she laughed. The way she said, "Oh my God, what?" She said it the same way Tommy Cray had said, "What do you think?" earlier at the pool.

Like I was slow.

I was 99 percent sure she was lying, and this made me madder than anything. Best friends aren't supposed to lie to each other. Not about boys.

That next week I ran into Maggie Daniels—Elaine O'Dea's second in command—in an aisle at Seller Brothers when I went to pick up some toilet paper and a couple of other things my mom had asked me to get. We were talking about how we didn't want to start back at school and catching up on all the gossip when Maggie said, "So what do you think about Mark Lopez and Alice?"

"What are you talking about?" I asked.

"Seriously? You don't know? I thought you guys were best friends."

"Well, yeah, we are, but I don't know what you're talking about," I said, nervous about seeming totally out of it.

"Just ask her about Mark Lopez," she said, "because he's telling everyone." She was laughing like she was in on a joke I wasn't. Which I guess she was.

I marched home, clutching the groceries, my candy cane–striped flip-flops flip-flopping on the sidewalk the whole way. I'd barely put the groceries away in the cupboard before I was texting Alice.

ran into maggie. what happened with mark l.?

Not two seconds later:

it was stupid.

what?

u can't tell anyone.

Just like always in Healy, everyone already knew, but I answered back:

u know i won't tell.

i'll be over in 2 sec.

"What?" I asked, yanking open the front door.

Alice's eyes darted around behind me.

"I'm home by myself," I said. "My dad's at work and my mom and sister are at some church thing."

Alice collapsed onto the family room couch and pulled her knees up to her chest.

"It was so dumb," she said. "I don't know why I did it."

"What?" I said, totally annoyed and envious at the same time.

Her voice dropped down low to a whisper.

"I gave him a blow job," she said.

"In the bathroom?" I said, whispering, too.

Alice nodded. I remember she tucked her hair behind her ears and gave me this look like she'd been caught cheating on a test she hadn't studied for. Half apologetic and half irritated with herself.

"It was just dumb," she said. "That's why I didn't tell you anything that night. It was just . . . it just happened. And we were drunk. I don't know. I mean, he wasn't my boyfriend or anything. And it's just . . . not that I'm saying that it was totally wrong or whatever. It was just . . . stupid."

"Didn't you do that with Tucker?" I asked, thinking of Alice losing her virginity freshman year. Alice slowly shook her head no and she looked down for a minute, staring at her hands. I wasn't sure how Alice felt, but there was a part of me that thought giving a blow job seemed like an even bigger deal than having sex. But if Alice felt that way, why did she give one to Mark when they weren't even dating? I wanted to ask, but I got the feeling Alice didn't want to keep talking about it.

"So, are you, like, hanging out with him now or something?" I said. I couldn't believe how jealous I felt. I knew what Alice had done was stupid and sort of slutty even, but I was jealous she had a story to tell and, once again, I didn't.

And I was mad. I was mad she had lied to me.

"He hasn't called me or anything since that night," Alice said, finally looking up. "And now he's left for UT."

That made me feel better. I know it sounds crappy to say, but it did.

"Well why'd you lie to me?" I asked.

Alice took a deep breath. She looked like she was picking out

49

her words really carefully. She got the same look when she was trying to figure out a math problem. "Kelsie, it's just . . . you know . . . you haven't, like . . . been with anyone . . . in that way. And that's . . . fine, okay? But . . . it's just, like . . . once you've had sex . . . I mean . . ."

"You lied to me because I'm a virgin?" I said. I gave her an insulted look because, well, I was insulted. She was talking to me like I was retarded or deaf or both. I was so mad I looked away and focused on the wall behind us. My mom had hung up a framed yellow sign that read "This is the day that the Lord has made. Let us rejoice and be glad in it! *Psalm 118, Verse 24.*" I wanted to throw something at that yellow sign.

"It's just . . . I mean . . ." Alice said.

"Forget it," I said. "Forget it."

I didn't, though. Not really.

After that, I don't think Alice ever hung out with Mark Lopez again, and I never really trusted Alice again. I mean, she was still my best friend, and we still spent most of tenth grade having sleepovers and staying up too late talking and texting people and blaming one another for our smelly farts and laughing so loud my dad would come down to the family room and start yelling at us to calm down and everything. And things were basically normal between us. The truth is, I still *liked* her.

But I can't say I trusted her.

Not 100 percent anymore.

I just kept thinking of how stupid I'd felt that night in the bed with her, Alice's room still stinking like Healy Pool North.

How she'd turned her face away from me. How she'd laughed at my guess about Mark. How she'd told me I wouldn't get it. And I guess I didn't.

Not then anyway.

I guess that's why when The Really Awful Stuff happened to me later, not long after Alice lied to me about Mark Lopez, I didn't tell her about it. Even if she was my best friend.

I guess that's why when all the rumors started about Alice this year it was so easy to let go of her. So easy to say goodbye. It was as easy as a buzzed, nighttime swim at Healy Pool North. As easy as remembering all the song lyrics in *Grease 2*. As easy as anything.

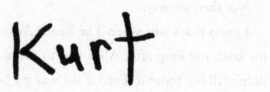

Kurt

I'VE BEEN WATCHING ALICE EVER SINCE THAT day I saw her sobbing on the bleachers outside of the school earlier this fall. I've wrestled with myself, attempting to find some way to speak with her. As I've mentioned, I don't talk to girls much, or to anyone at school, really, and this state, while unusual to many, seems natural to me. I do make an exception for Mr. Becker, my Physics teacher. He is one of the few teachers at Healy High who seems more interested in the subject matter at hand than what is happening on the football field or at the pep rallies. I often wonder how someone like Mr. Becker ended up staying in Healy, not married, living in a garage apartment behind his sister's house (even though I'm sure he could afford something nicer). He certainly is a good-enough instructor to move on to a bigger city school somewhere. Earn more money. Teach more advanced students.

He and I were sitting in his messy classroom yesterday afternoon discussing quantum gravity. Because of the Halloween holiday, everyone in Healy High had cleared out early to prepare for a night of debauchery and pranks. Everyone but me, of course. At one moment during our discussion, the conversation waned a bit, and I asked him why he hadn't moved somewhere else.

"It's such a pleasure to teach you, to talk with you," he answered. "You have a gifted mind." He leaned back in his chair, his arms behind his head, and I could see the yellowing stains on his shirt, under his arms. If Mr. Becker knew they were there, he didn't seem to care. Nor did he seem to care that he was almost completely bald and had pockmarks on his cheeks from bad acne, or that he had several unknowable stains on his tie.

I have a gifted mind, all right. I know enough to know that I do not want to turn out like Mr. Becker. And I know enough to know that to ask Mr. Becker about how to talk to Alice would be more complicated than discussing quantum gravity. I get the sense Mr. Becker doesn't know how to talk to girls either.

Girls were still on my mind as I exited Mr. Becker's room after school. Well, truth be told there was only one girl on my mind, and as I stepped out into the hallway magically there she was, as alive and real and beautiful as she is in all of my dreams. Alice Franklin. She was standing in the doorway of Mr. Commons's classroom, her lovely frame covered in that bulky sweatshirt. Only she didn't have the hood pulled up as she often does, and her gamine haircut caught my eye first. Her neck was so amazingly swanlike I had to look away.

I tried to make myself seem preoccupied by leaning down and tying my shoe. Such a predictable move, I realize, but it worked in that I was able to listen as Mr. Commons spoke aggressively with Alice about a paper she was holding in her hand.

"No, there is no extra credit in my class, Alice," he was saying as I untied my tied shoe and retied it again. "I realize a 63 is going to kill your average, sweetheart, but you need to focus more in class." Mr. Commons did not say the word *sweetheart* in a comforting, reassuring manner. Rather, the way he said it reminded me of a mob boss in a bad movie. It was condescending.

"Okay, fine," Alice said, her voice small with only a trace of spunk or life left in it. I waited for Mr. Commons to offer help or tutoring, but I knew that wasn't going to happen. When I took his Algebra II class as a freshman, he thought it was fun to make me go up to the board and teach the subject's basic principles so he could relax at his desk. (I'm certain that piece of information makes it quite clear why I have no friends at Healy High.) I even waited for Mr. Commons to address the possibility that what had happened to Alice this year was having an impact on her grades. That perhaps becoming The Slut Who Killed the Star Quarterback was making it difficult to focus on her studies. But he didn't mention it. I'm sure he knew about it. But I doubt he cared. Maybe he was even glad Alice was failing his class. After all, he is one of the assistants to the football coach.

Alice walked past me. I remained bent over like a deformed hobgoblin maniacally focused on its shoe. I don't know if she even realized I was there, but that night, sitting in my bedroom, I got an idea. It came to me in such a rush—in as much of a rush as my thoughts about quantum gravity and game theory come to me—but this thought was much more exciting. It was the thought that could change everything.

But I had to ask myself—did I want to change everything? In truth I was quite happy with things the way they were. Perhaps the better word would be *satisfied*. I had worked out a system of living in Healy that provided me with a relatively calm existence where I was mostly left alone to do as I wished, and I enjoyed that peaceful sense of being. Sure, I had experienced the clichés of high school life that someone of my social standing is usually forced to endure—jocks calling me a nerd in the hallways or making perverted gestures at me when I spoke in class, pretty girls rolling their eyes when I asked too many questions of the teacher—but over time even those elements of my life had faded as the community simply became accustomed to me and I to them. I was Kurt Morelli, space alien from another planet who had been granted temporary residency in their world. I had my routines: my evenings were spent reading or chatting online about science and literature with some of the university students and professors from my coursework, my Saturday afternoons watching history documentaries with my grandmother. And there was even Mr. Becker to chat with at school. In another year and a half I would be gone and in college. Why change anything?

And then I remembered Alice Franklin's tremendous knees

and beautiful face and the way she cried on the bleachers after school that day. And I remembered everything I knew about her. I remembered until my comfortable cocoon started to feel slightly claustrophobic, and I knew I simply had to follow through with my idea before I chickened out. So before I lost the little nerve I had, I ripped a piece of paper out of a notebook and spent an hour drafting until I wrote the following:

> Alice,
> I'm wondering if you would be interested
> in some tutoring help in Algebra II. I
> remember helping you with your Geometry
> homework last year, and I thought perhaps
> you'd still like the help. If so, just let me
> know. I'm happy to assist you as math is
> one of my strongest subjects.
> > Sincerely,
> > Kurt Morelli

This morning I folded the paper in half and slid it through the vent in Alice's locker. And I began to wait.

Elaine

I KNOW I'M PRETTY. I'M NOT GORGEOUS LIKE some movie star, but I'm pretty. I'm noticeable. I've got long, dark blond hair that I don't have to wash every day, and it still turns out nice. (Of course I still wash it every day.) I have green eyes, which make me stand out in a cool way instead of a weird way. I'm 5'5" which seems like the perfect height for a girl, because I'm not going to tower over some guy but I'm also not going to be so short that a basketball player feels weird asking me out. And my skin has always been really clear to the point where I'm actually sort of freaked out that I'm going to wake up one morning with fifty enormous zits on my face just because I'm overdue.

The one thing is my body. I'm curvy. I've got sort of big boobs (not crazy big or whatever, but big enough that by fifth grade I definitely needed a bra). My butt is sort of big, too, or I guess you would say it's really round, but in my best moments I don't really think that's such a bad thing. I actually think I have a pretty good body.

I mean, if I didn't, I don't think I would have so many boys always wanting to ask me out or come to my parties. Including The Party.

It was actually sort of a last-minute thing, and months later I still think about how everything that happened this fall happened because of this random party I never even anticipated throwing. Even that afternoon, I wasn't planning on throwing one. I walked downstairs to find something to eat and I found my mother in the kitchen, staring into the refrigerator like she was waiting for the orange juice to talk back.

"Elaine," she said, pulling out a plastic bag full of grapes (Weight Watchers points=0) and digging around for some, "you know what I'm thinking?"

I rolled my eyes because I totally knew what was coming.

"You want to join Weight Watchers again," I told her.

"How did you guess?" she said, which is so ridiculous because how could I not guess? Every time my mother stares into the refrigerator like a prisoner of war about to be shot, it's time to go back to Weight Watchers. Every time my mother whines about her jeans being too tight, it's time to go back to Weight Watchers. Every time we order a pizza and my mother picks up a third slice and then puts it down and then picks it back up and eats it with a frown on her face, it's time to go back to Weight Watchers.

If my mother goes back to Weight Watchers, I have to go back to Weight Watchers. It's been that way since I was fourteen, and I hate it.

My mother has lost the same twenty pounds so many times I could make an entire extra mom out of all the pounds if I added them up. I've lost the same ten pounds just as many times, and I knew from the way my mom was staring at those grapes what was coming. Meetings on Saturday mornings where I have to sit and listen to some old lady talk about her Greek yogurt (Weight Watchers points = 3) or how she can't find time to work out even though she's totally retired. Weighing in behind a curtain and trying to hold my breath in case it makes me weigh less. Calculating the points of everything I eat so that I can't even look at a Snickers bar without doing high-level algebra (Weight Watchers points = 8).

Then my mom will take all our special Weight Watchers food and use a black Sharpie to label it with point values and store it on one shelf in the fridge and one shelf in the cabinet, and if she's feeling totally nuts, she might even put a Post-it note on the shelves that says "MOM'S AND ELAINE'S SPECIAL FOOD—DON'T TOUCH!" which is totally stupid seeing as the only other person who lives in the house is my dad and he wouldn't touch our SPECIAL FOOD even if it meant the Healy Tigers were guaranteed a winning football season for the rest of his natural life.

"So, honey, will you come with me?" my mother asked. "This time I know I'm gonna keep it off."

I poured myself a huge bowl of corn flakes and then went to the sugar bowl and dumped half of it on top of my cereal (Weight Watchers points = Who freaking cares).

"Mom, do I have to?"

"Elaine, it's so much more fun when we go together, you know that. And you want to watch your figure, too, babe. Dance squad is starting up again in the fall, and you don't want to look funny in your uniform in front of everyone."

Funny as in fat.

"Okay," I said, and I jammed a spoonful of milk and sugar into my mouth and let all the sugar dissolve, like a real slow goodbye.

Then my mom told me she and my dad were going over to her sister's place in Dove Lake for dinner and they'd just end up spending the night and did I want to come? Which meant she and my dad were probably going to drink too many beers and wouldn't want to drive the twenty miles back to Healy.

"No, I think I'll just stay here. Can I have some people over?"

My mother popped a grape into her mouth and eyed me.

"You mean like a party?"

"No, I mean like people."

My mom isn't dumb. True, she's given Weight Watchers so much money it probably could have paid for my college education by now, but she's not dumb about most things. She went to Healy High and she knows there isn't anything to do around here except drive to the Healy High parking lot and drink beer, so maybe she figured it would be better if we just drank the beer in our living room.

"Elaine, I just don't want it to get too crazy, okay? And nobody goes into the bedrooms. This is strictly a family room and kitchen affair. And nobody leaves drunk."

"Okay, fine," I said, and I knew she knew she owed me one because I was going to do Weight Watchers with her again.

I finished my cereal and went upstairs and texted the usual suspects and told them to come over around nine o'clock that night and invite whoever, and I figured out who could get alcohol. I talked on the phone with some of my girlfriends about what to wear, I texted Kelsie Sanders back and told her not to worry if she was too sick to make it because it would probably be boring anyway, and I read Brandon Fitzsimmons's texts asking me if I had enough beer lined up. I texted back that we could always use more, then briefly entertained the idea of messing around with him at the party. We were totally off again at that point, but still, sometimes it was just fun to mess around. I really couldn't understand how my mother thought I was too fat when I had a serious history with the hottest and most popular guy in the school. Besides, guys like curvy girls. It always says so in *Glamour*.

By 9:30 p.m. everyone was there. By everyone I mostly mean the twenty to thirty people in the upcoming junior class and the twenty to thirty people in the upcoming senior class who were cool enough to be invited to my party. There were also a handful of former Healy High students who were heading back to college in a couple of days, so that's why Tommy Cray was there. And, last and certainly least, there were a few token upcoming sophomores who were probably the coolest kids in *their* class, which is why they were invited to my party, and they were sitting around sort of nervously sipping their beers like they couldn't believe they were actually lucky enough to be there.

"Elaine, where do your parents keep the whiskey?" Josh Waverly said to me from the kitchen. I could only hear his voice, not see him.

"They don't drink whiskey," I said, which is a lie. I'd taken all the hard liquor and hidden it in the attic. If I didn't want my mom to kill me, we had to stick to the cans of Natty Light and Bud Light that people stole from their parents' refrigerators.

"Aw, Elaine, you know you're lying. Where did you hide the whiskey?" Josh whined. "I really need some whiskey." You could tell he was already kind of drunk.

"You need to get laid," Brandon Fitzsimmons said from the couch where he was drinking his fourth beer. For a second I remembered the first time we did it in my room during winter break of tenth grade. Even now I remember everything cute about him. How he was so cut, clear skinned, clear eyed, with that perfect jock attitude that I love. Like he could win the Super Bowl and make out with me for hours in the same day.

"What the hell do you know about getting laid?" some dumb

sophomore football player said, walking into the room with no shirt on and fat-free Reddi-wip sprayed all over his bare chest in the shape of a penis. I mean he had honest to God squirted on balls and a big dick right there on his chest. (Weight Watchers points for fat-free Reddi-wip = 0!)

"Oh my God," my friend Maggie said, hiding under a throw pillow, but you could tell she was loving it just like everyone at the party.

As for me, I had a couple of beers—enough that I was buzzed but not wasted, having fun but not totally out of control. I wandered from kitchen to living room to backyard deck, talking to people and getting the latest gossip and going to get another beer, etc. At one point I spotted Alice Franklin in the corner with Brandon. She was sitting on his lap and laughing. I mean, honestly. Sitting on his lap? For a split second I remembered the eighth grade dance when Brandon and I had been *on again* and I'd found out the two of them were fooling around in the coat closet. Tonight she was wearing a tight raspberry T-shirt that made her raspberry lips look brighter and her perfect boobs look bigger. Alice was just as pretty as she had been in eighth grade. Prettier, actually.

I wanted to smack her.

I pushed her and Brandon out of my mind and drank another beer. I followed Maggie out to the porch and took a drag of someone's cigarette. It was getting late when I decided I should try to keep an eye on what was going on upstairs. It was actually turning into a pretty crowded party even if it wasn't approaching teen movie party status, and I was freaking out that people would end up having sex in my parents' bedroom. Before everyone arrived, I'd shut the door and taped a sign on it that said "STAY OUT OR YOU'LL NEVER GET INVITED TO ANOTHER PARTY," but signs don't always work with drunk people.

Upstairs was cool and quiet compared to the level of noise downstairs. The floorboards squeaked under the new carpet my parents had put in all the bedrooms at the beginning of the summer. The chemical smell was still hanging in the air. I knocked on my parents' bedroom door and then slowly opened it. Empty and dark. Their bed was made up nice and neat, and the hall light shone onto my mom's stack of *O* magazines sitting carefully on her nightstand.

Then I heard voices coming from my room. I headed down the hall and opened it without knocking this time, and I saw Brandon Fitzsimmons sitting on my bed. Standing next to the bed was Alice Franklin. She had this weird, uncomfortable look on her face.

"Hey, Elaine," she said with this little gasp, like she was wishing I hadn't just walked in on her.

Then I noticed Brandon was holding a notebook open on his lap, and he was reading from it with a smirk on his face.

"When I had to start wearing a bra in fifth grade, my mom told me it was a blessing," he read out loud in a sing-song voice, like he was trying to sound like a girl. "My butt is pretty round,

I know, but I think I look good in clothes." Then he looked up from the book to my face. "Damn, girl, I know that's true. But you look good without them, too."

Brandon was reading from my diary—the black-and-white composition book I keep under the mattress. Usually. Only I must have left it out or he found it or something because he was reading from it. Out loud. In front of Alice. In front of me.

My off-again, on-again, off-again guy—the guy I had lost my virginity to—was reading about my fat butt.

Brandon continued, "I've gotten naked in front of the mirror and really looked at myself, and I don't think I look bad that way either."

Oh my God.

"Give me that!" I screamed, and I reached for it, but Brandon grabbed my wrist and wrestled me to the bed. He was so strong he could hold me down with one hand and still keep the open book in the other.

"I know I have big boobs but so do all the women in our family, including my mom," he read, his eyebrows popping. "Your mom has big tits? I'll have to look next time!" He was laughing that big, loud, so-sure-of-himself jock laugh that I normally loved but right then made me sick. He tossed the book aside and pinned me down, his hands on my wrists, his knees pressing up along my outer thighs. I couldn't move if I tried. I'd done it with him here, on this very bed, and that had been nice. Sweet even. But this Brandon was scary as hell.

"Let me check out your big tits," he said, gasping for air. "You know I've seen 'em before." He was totally, ridiculously drunk. His face was super red, and little drops of sweat were seeping out around his hairline. And Alice Franklin was just standing there next to us like she'd paid to watch a show or something.

Finally she said, "Brandon, let's just go." Her voice sounded really small and embarrassed.

Brandon looked me in the eyes, and for the tiniest, weirdest second they were just . . . empty. Like there was nothing there. No emotion, no feeling, nothing. And then a second after that it was like he'd decided I'd bored him or something. He pushed off of me and stood up, the bed bouncing under me once or twice, the coils of my mattress squeaking like mice.

"Come on, Elaine," he said, his trademark cute football player face returning. "You know I love you, sweetheart."

"Elaine, I'm sorry," Alice said, and she leaned over and picked up my notebook which Brandon had thrown on the floor.

"What is this?" I said, taking the notebook and motioning at the two of them with disgust. "Eighth grade part two?" Brandon stumbled out of the room, taking Alice's hand, and she followed him.

I stayed in my room for what felt like forever, completely and totally too embarrassed to go downstairs. What if Brandon and Alice told everybody what I'd written? I took my diary and jammed it in my closet on the top shelf, hiding it under the box of report cards and school projects my mom had made me keep. I never wanted to see it again.

I kept waiting for someone to come up and find me, but not even any of my best girlfriends did. I must have nodded off or something because suddenly I woke up and looked at the clock: 12:45 a.m. Shit. I said a quick little prayer that the downstairs wasn't trashed.

It was. There were bottles and cans everywhere, and I could see a corner by the television where someone had spilled an entire can of beer and hadn't even tried to clean it up. My head was totally pounding and my entire body felt fuzzy.

I decided I'd never have another party.

"Where were you?" my friend Maggie said from the corner of the couch where she was curled up, her head in Josh Waverly's lap. Josh was fooling around with his phone. There were a few other kids around, most of them sipping what was left of the beer or sleeping or watching MTV on low volume.

I saw Brandon Fitzsimmons sitting on the floor, his back against a wall, his phone in his lap. He was still wasted, his eyes staring out at nothing. Alice wasn't anywhere to be seen.

"I fell asleep," I said, picking up a few bottles to take to the kitchen. "Y'all are gonna have to leave or help me clean up."

As I headed for the trash, I heard a yelp from Josh Waverly.

"Are you serious, dude?!"

I carefully placed the bottles on top of the mountain of bottles already in the trash can and headed back into the living room. Josh was looking at his phone and then looked across the room at Brandon, who had half a grin pasted on his face. He shot his eyebrows up twice, real quick.

Josh asked something again about Brandon being serious.

Brandon shot his eyebrows up twice again and grinned all the way this time.

"What the hell?" Maggie said, and she reached up from Josh's lap and grabbed his phone to see what had caught Josh's attention. Then she called Brandon a pervert.

"What are you freaking out about?" I asked, and I glanced over Josh's shoulder at the text that had just arrived from Brandon.

tommy and me banged alice franklin upstairs.

That was all it said. Seven words that would change everything.

I read the text from Brandon again.

tommy and me banged alice franklin upstairs.

"Who went first?" Josh asked with a snort, and for a second I thought Josh was grossed out, but then he grinned at Brandon like Brandon had just thrown him a touchdown pass.

"Dude! Like you even have to ask?" Brandon answered, holding both his arms out wide like he was preparing to accept all the praise he had coming to him.

Maggie rolled her eyes and she pulled out her phone to

start texting. All of Healy High would know what was up by sunrise.

By the time school started a few weeks later, it was all everyone talked about. How Alice Franklin slept with two guys in one night in my guest bedroom. Two guys in one HOUR. The thought of it was enough to make me want to puke. Honestly, what kind of girl does that?

I just kept picturing her at the party, sitting in Brandon's lap and looking all perfect, and I kept picturing her standing there next to Brandon as he read from my diary, her skinny, cute body with the amazing boobs and butt. She was probably totally enjoying making fun of me when Brandon found the notebook. I could picture her making him read it out loud. And then she actually pretended to be sorry when I walked in. She even picked it up off the floor and gave it back to me.

And then she went and did it with two dudes in one night.

Seriously. Here's a girl who messes around with a guy when that guy is *on again* with another girl, and here's a girl who sleeps with two guys in one night, and here's a girl who messes around with random dudes at the pool. I mean, it's like she's just this insult to girls.

And even though she acted like nothing was up, how could she NOT have known everyone was talking about her behind her back? I mean, even the incoming freshmen knew what went down.

Dude, did you hear about that junior girl Alice and the two guys at that party?

That junior girl Alice slept with Brandon Fitzsimmons and that other guy this summer.

OMG that Alice Franklin girl is so slutty!

Even the adults started talking about it. One Saturday when we were on the way home from another Weight Watchers meeting, my mom turned to me when we were at a stoplight and all of a sudden asked, "I keep hearing these stories about Alice Franklin. Are they true?"

"That girl is a total slut," I said.

My mom gripped the wheel and told me not to use that word, but then she started asking me all these questions, and I told her what I could. I thought my mom was going to be really pissed that all this went down in our house, but you could tell she was way more interested in what everybody was saying about Alice and did Alice's mom know and blah blah blah.

At the Weight Watchers meeting she'd gained two pounds, so maybe she just wanted to take her mind off everything with some super crazy gossip, but I had a feeling my mom would have been interested even if she hadn't gained weight.

And then Brandon Fitzsimmons died.

The news that Brandon died spread faster than the news about Alice, and the news that he crashed his car because Alice was sending him gross texts spread even faster than that. Nobody knew what the texts said exactly, but we figured they were disgusting and they were desperate, and of course they had to be both of those things because they were coming from Alice Franklin, who didn't come to school for a week after the news got out about what she had done.

Healy High freaked out after Brandon died—everyone was crying in the hallways and the English teachers tried to get us to write about our emotions and everyone wore ribbons with the school colors for, I don't know, a week. They brought in grief counselors, and the next game against Dominion was, like, mandatory attendance for the entire town. They hung a banner reading "BRANDON FITZSIMMONS * HEALY HIGH TIGER FOREVER" at the front entrance of the stadium, and Brandon's parents came out onto the field during halftime and announced the Brandon Fitzsimmons Scholarship Fund, and Josh Waverly was in his uniform on the sidelines even though he couldn't play yet. Even the players from Dominion bowed their heads during the moment of silence, and it was almost like they let us win. Like they knew how bad it would look if we lost to them.

Alice came back to school eventually, of course.

It was weird how we were all sort of connected after Brandon died—the ribbons with the school colors, the moment of silence at the all-school assembly, the stories in the paper that people cut out and put up in their lockers. Even after all of that sort of calmed down, people still needed something to hang on to. I mean, things were kinda back to normal—the cafeteria ladies asked us if we wanted a fruit cup or a yogurt, the janitors dumped the pink powder on top of people's puke, the teachers gave out their boring homework assignments and their pop quizzes about nothing we'll ever actually need in real life—but I think people needed something that made them feel, I don't know . . . like we were all still in it together.

So we picked on Alice Franklin. A nobody, a slut, a killer.

And then the craziest thing happened this afternoon. Maggie and me and some of our other girlfriends were sitting in the bathroom cutting French class or Chemistry class or whatever class we had that period. I was sort of trying not to think about the fact that I was starving because I'd only had a granola bar for lunch. Kelsie Sanders was with us. Now I could sort of tell that Kelsie was feeling really super tentative about hanging out with us—I mean, she was Alice's best friend. I think she was worried that maybe we wouldn't accept her, but Kelsie's always been cool with me. She's always been super sweet and everything. You could just tell, though, that she was thinking that any second we were going to tell her to get lost. Like the way she hesitated before talking. Or the way she laughed a little too hard at everything I said. It's weird, the feeling of power you get sometimes when you're popular, but I guess I try to use my power for good, not evil. So I've been letting Kelsie Sanders hang out with us.

Anyway, so this afternoon we were all sitting there talking about whatever when Kelsie suddenly said all dramatically, "Okay, so I have to tell you something. About Alice."

"What, she did it with the entire football team last weekend?" I said, fishing in my purse for my lipstick.

"No, it's way worse. I think she got an . . . abortion."

Kelsie lowered her voice to a whisper when she said the word *abortion*. I let my lipstick drop.

"What the hell?" I said, and before I could say anything else, Maggie said, "Oh God, did your mom make you protest again?" Maggie goes to the same totally whacked-out church as Kelsie, so I guess she figured out what was up.

"Yes," Kelsie said, rolling her eyes. She told us how her mom was always dragging her and her little sister to the Women's Care Clinic in the city to protest abortion and how she tried to get out of it whenever she could, but on some Saturdays she found herself standing by the gate of the clinic, holding up posters.

"Like, ones with dead babies on them?" somebody said, and Kelsie shuddered a little and said yes.

"So, what? You saw her go into the clinic?" I asked.

"Yeah," Kelsie said. "Last weekend. With her mom. She didn't see me. They just rushed in there."

"Well, maybe she was just going for a checkup?" Maggie asked.

I arched an eyebrow. "Like they don't have doctors in Healy who do checkups?" Naturally, everyone agreed with me.

"Do you think it was from . . . that night?" someone else asked.

"Do the math," I said. "My party was what, close to three months ago? Perfect timing. I'm sure it was from that night."

"And the really gross and scary thing is . . ." Kelsie continued, and for a second I could see how much she was loving this, just getting to be in the center of our little group with all of us listening to her. ". . . I mean, she would have no idea who the father is. Tommy or Brandon? Isn't that so totally skanky?"

"Totally," Maggie whispered.

"I can't even believe she used to be my friend," Kelsie said. "It's just, like, that was another time in my life, you know?"

"Totally," I said.

"So you don't miss her?" Maggie asked. "You don't even feel a little sorry for her?" I thought Maggie was acting weird. I mean, Alice was responsible for Brandon Fitzsimmons dying. And it wasn't like Alice *had* to sleep with him at my party.

What Kelsie did next really surprised me. We were just standing there in that girls' bathroom with the green and white tile and the scummy sinks and instead of answering Maggie, Kelsie searched through her bag until she found a black Sharpie, and she opened up the stall next to us, the middle one. She uncapped the marker and wrote right there on the wall to the left of the toilet in letters that were at least two inches high.

ATTENTION!

ALICE FRANKLIN IS A HO SLUT WHORE WHO DOES IT WITH EVERYBODY!!!

We all laughed, all of us, and then I said, "My turn."

ALICE FRANKLIN HAS GIVEN 423 BLOW JOBS!!! NOW THAT'S A LOT OF DICK!

I stared at the graffiti and watched how quickly the shiny Sharpie writing dulled into a permanent black stain. The other girls behind me lined up to take their turns.

JOSH

I'VE BEEN THINKING ABOUT THE ACCIDENT pretty much all the time. The sounds of the ambulance. The sun beating down on me as they pulled me out of the car. How it's really true that time speeds up and slows down and your brain goes all whacked out in moments like a car wreck. I wouldn't say I think about it constantly, but basically I think about it pretty much a lot. I think about Officer Daniels interviewing me in the hospital. I think about Mrs. Fitzsimmons sitting on my dad's recliner asking me all those questions.

It's weird, the things I think about when I remember the wreck and everything that happened afterward. Like maybe my brain is trying to make it so I don't think about what happened right before the accident and Brandon's dying. It just focuses on the stupid stuff instead. Like Officer Daniels's chewed-up pencil. Or Mrs. Fitzsimmons's glass of sweet tea.

But I still think about it. I think about it during football games (we lost our last one against Johnston) and I think about it while eating mystery meat in the cafeteria and I think about it in English class. We've been reading a book about the olden days when this lady supposedly did it with some guy and they weren't married and she had his baby, and that was a huge deal back then. So she had to wear a red letter *A* on her dress all the time. Kind of messed up, I guess.

I think about it until I can't think about it in any new kind of way. Until my brain gives out and goes fuzzy or blank.

Sometimes I think about the ride home from Elaine O'Dea's famous party. The one where Alice did what she did. Anyway, Elaine made this big deal about me not driving home drunk. I think she promised her parents, but I just wanted to go. After that text about Alice, it just felt like it was time to leave. Brandon kind of mumbled could I give him a lift? Could he crash at my place? "Okay," I said.

He was so wasted I had to help him into the car. Sometimes, when my brain remembers this night, it remembers little things, too. Like Brandon smelling of booze, and the prickle of his stubble rubbing against my face as I tried to hold him up and get him into my dad's Chevy S-10. And the way he kept laughing at everything even when nothing was funny.

Anyway, I was drunk, but he was way drunker, and that's why I was the one to drive us back to my house.

Healy is a dead zone after midnight. Sonic, McDonald's, Walgreens, the Curl Up and Dye, Auto Zone, the Healy Advocate, the Sno-Cone Shop, Burger King, Wendy's, Chick-fil-A: no lights on in any of them. Nobody walking anywhere; hardly any other cars. Not even the Walmart in Healy is open twenty-four hours. Drunk driving late at night is pretty safe around here, I guess.

Making our way home, I looked over at Brandon, and he was slumped against the passenger window. But his glassy eyes were open.

"Did you really do it?" I asked.

"Do what?" he said, kind of slurry.

"You and Tommy Cray . . . and Alice."

Brandon got this smirk like he was getting some image back in his head.

"Yeah, we really did it, man," he answered me. "Fuckin' awesome, too. Alice is hot. Even with that short hair and shit." He started laughing again as he rambled on.

"Tommy didn't mind sloppy seconds?" I asked, kind of not wanting to ask but asking anyway.

"No he didn't," Brandon said. "She couldn't get enough. Me twice and Tommy once. I'm gonna have to hit that again soon." He yawned so wide I heard his jaw pop.

We got home, and my mom and dad and brother were all asleep. A good thing, I thought to myself as I helped Brandon down to the floor of my bedroom. I gave him an extra pillow. Sophomore year at school, they had this guy come in and talk to us about alcohol and drug abuse, and the guy said you should always put a drunk person on his side, so he doesn't choke on his own vomit. I guess the principal got mad at that later on because he thought the comment encouraged drinking, but it's the only thing I remember from that whole speech.

Brandon was passed out, so I sort of squatted down on my knees and got behind him. I tucked my hands under his back and rolled him over. Brandon had muscles all over. I could feel them under his red-and-white Healy Tigers T-shirt. It was easy to see why the girls were all hot for him.

So I was on my knees, Brandon was on his side, and I stayed there. I stared at the back of his neck where his hair was growing together into a point, right in the center of his neck. His hair was short, brown, sort of curly. I put a finger right there, right at the back of his neck. And I touched his hair. First one finger. Then two. Then my whole hand was touching the back of his neck and his hair. I mean, I was so wasted. But I touched. His hair was softer than it looked. A lot softer. The light from the street lamp outside my window lit up his whole face. It was that perfect kind of face you see on guys who pose for aftershave ads in magazines. I don't know if Brandon had any idea how good looking he really was.

His breathing was slow, and for a second I worried maybe it was too slow. Then I worried what the hell Brandon would do if he woke up and saw my hand on his neck, touching his hair like some weirdo. I pulled my hand away real fast and stood up. I stared at him for a while, maybe for as long as a few minutes. The ground sort of rocked under my feet like it does when you're drunk and tired. Then I pulled my shirt and jeans off and got into bed. The next morning, I didn't remember falling asleep.

The other day some of the guys from the team and me snuck into this girls' bathroom on the second floor when we were supposed to be in Study Hall. There was some freshman chick in there just washing her hands when we walked in; she walked out real fast because she knew why we were there.

"Check this out," one of the guys said, pushing open the door.

Alice likes it fast and hard.

Alice did it with my grandpa. And she liked it!

RIP Fitzsimmons! Alice Franklin = Killer/Whore

Flush if you've done Alice.

"Man," I said, not sure what to think. I mean, it was pretty crazy just the amount of graffiti. You could see one part where maybe the janitors had tried to clean it and then given up. It was everywhere, all over the place.

"Some of the girls started it, man," one of the guys said, laughing. "Like a week ago. But check it out. It's totally everywhere."

Alice Franklin is a whore, slut, ho, bitch, and a killer, too!!!

It's the slut's fault!

Screw you, Alice! Healy Tiger #35 FOREVER.

I thought about the accident again, but my brain wouldn't let me replay it. It just kept jumping all over the place. I could hear Mrs. Fitzsimmons's voice in my head.

"So you could say she was distracting him with her texts?" Mrs. Fitzsimmons asked.

"Yeah," I answered. "You could say he was distracted."

My mind sort of jumped back to grade school, to the fourth grade, when I used to sit behind Alice and throw really small wads of paper at her hair just to annoy her. But it was all funny back then. Alice used to turn her head and roll her eyes at me, but then she would just laugh, this loud, crazy laugh she has, and I would try to look all innocent like I didn't know what she was so upset about.

And then I would laugh, too.

Then my head was back in that stall, looking at the graffiti.

"Add something," one of the guys said, handing me a Sharpie. He'd already taken the cap off.

I tried to think of something, but I just kept thinking of those little white wads of balled-up lined paper sitting in Alice's real dark hair. Her hair was longer back then.

"Come on, man, hurry up. We gotta get out of here," somebody else said.

Finally it came to me, and I put down *Alice did Dallas.* All the other guys laughed and they were happy it rhymed.

Later on, when I was hanging out in front of the school with some of my buddies, I saw Alice walking home alone, buried in that sweatshirt. You couldn't see her dark hair since she had her hood up. I looked at her for a few seconds, but I don't think she ever saw me. Anyway I hope she didn't.

Kurt

NOT VERY LONG AFTER I SLIPPED THE NOTE
into Alice's locker, she approached me at mine. It was the end of
the day, and I was packing up my numerous books and note-
books and the like into my backpack, and I looked up and there
was Alice, standing to my left, holding the note I left her.

"What's this about?" she said, holding the paper up. She did
not seem pleased. Her eyebrows sort of twitched and knit together over her beautiful dark brown eyes.

I couldn't look at her face. It was too gorgeous. But if I
couldn't look at her face, how would I be able to help her with
Algebra II?

"I was simply, um, offering my help. I felt like perhaps you
could use that help in your math class." I sounded like a robot.
No, I sounded like a socially illiterate imbecile robot, which I
suppose I can be at times. Especially the socially illiterate part.

The hood was down on her sweatshirt. Her short, elfin hair was tucked behind her ears. I forced myself to try and make eye contact, but I could only focus on the bottom half of her face. Her full lips looked like two fresh raspberries, one sitting on top of the other. I noticed a small freckle or two under her bottom lip.

She is perfection. She is a gumdrop. She is everything.

"But *why* are you offering your help?" Alice said. She sounded accusatory, angry. And who could blame her?

"I just . . ." I muttered. There was no way I could explain about overhearing her conversation with Mr. Commons without sounding like a stalker. But what other reason could I give? My own unending crush on her?

"You just what?" she said. And for a moment, just a slight sliver of time, I sensed she was more bewildered than annoyed. More perplexed than agitated.

"I just want to help you," I said, shutting my locker and forcing myself to look her in the eyes. "With math."

And then the most incredible thing happened. After what seemed like an eternity, Alice Franklin nodded and said, "Okay." She said this and I felt the floor of Healy High School give out underneath me.

"Do you, like, want to come over to my house?" she added. "Or should I come over to your place?"

"I'll come over if that would be easier for you," I answered with no real thought—it was simply the first response that came out of my mouth. Alice scribbled down her address on a corner of my Physics notebook. I noticed her long and lean fingers as she gripped the pencil.

Even her fingers are perfect.

5530 Robindell, she wrote. Her letters were bubbly and girlish. Her handwriting made her seem happier than she actually was.

"When should we meet?" I asked.

Alice Franklin put her pencil back in her bag.

"What about tonight? Eight o'clock?"

It was a Friday night, but I had no plans, and I suppose Alice Franklin didn't either.

"All right," I said. "I'll be there."

My grandmother loaned me her car to drive over to Alice's house. When I told her who I was tutoring, her face flinched with a bit of recognition. Even my grandmother knows about Alice Franklin. Now that should tell you something. No doubt she learned about her at a prayer meeting when some sweet, gossipy Healy soul suggested praying for the town's most wayward girl, but to her credit she didn't say anything when I mentioned going over to Alice Franklin's house. She just handed me the keys and reminded me to go easy on the clutch.

I don't know how I walked from the car to the house, which is a small pink and white bungalow in what some might consider the rougher section of town. But somehow I made the journey. There was a flowerpot full of cigarette butts on the porch just outside the front door, and I wondered if it was Alice who smoked or Mrs. Franklin. Make that Ms. Franklin. Biologically, Alice has a father of course. But if a Mr. Franklin has ever walked the streets of Healy, no one has ever seen him do it.

My hand formed a fist and knocked on the door, and there was Alice, present before me with a neutral expression on her face. No smile, no hello. She just swung open the door and stood there in her dark blue jeans and a black T-shirt. No sweatshirt for once. The T-shirt had a high neck, I noticed. For this I was grateful.

"Hey," she said, and I sensed she was wary. "Come in."

I followed her to the brightly lit kitchen where she had her Algebra II textbook and a pink spiral notebook set out on the table next to a row of freshly sharpened yellow pencils. She sat down in front of them and motioned for me to take the seat at the head of the table so we were sitting catty-corner across from one another. I wondered if Alice's mom was going to come out from somewhere, and Alice must have read my mind because she said, "My mom isn't here. She's out on a date."

"Oh," I said.

"Do you want something to drink? I have Coke and orange juice and water."

Here was Alice Franklin, the most beautiful girl in Healy. Here she was allowing me into her house, offering me something to drink. I swallowed hard and said, "A Coke, please." She got herself one, too.

After a few sips from a cold can, Alice opened up her notebook and showed me her current assignment. It was baby stuff for me, and I picked up a pencil and started working problems for her. I narrated as I worked, talking out the problems as slowly as I could. I talked about the binomials and the radicals as if they were intimate friends of mine whom I hadn't talked to in some time. Soon I found myself lost in the graphs and slopes and polynomials. Alice interrupted me as I worked to ask a question or two, and I stopped and explained. Every so often she said, "Oh. *Oh.* Mr. Commons never made it make sense like that." Eventually, I handed her a pencil and our fingers touched, and then I watched as she carefully graphed a curve.

"That's right!" I told her, excited.

"It is?" she said, glancing up at me only briefly before going back to finish the sloping upward line. Like if she looked away for too long she'd make an error somehow.

"Yes!" I told her.

"Wow," she said, finally putting down the pencil. She looked at me and for an instant she smiled a true, genuine smile. I noticed one of her incisors was a little crooked. Just a little.

"Want to try another one?" I asked, and Alice did, and she got that problem right, too.

"It looks like you might not need my help that much after all," I said, desperate to say something and then instantly regretting what I had just said. If she didn't need my help (which, despite two correct problems, she so clearly *did*), then how would I see her again?

My comment did something to Alice. Her smile disappeared, and perhaps I'm exaggerating, but I think she frowned. Ever so slightly.

"You want to *sleep with me*, don't you?" Alice said, shutting her Algebra II textbook. You might even say she slammed it. "You think I'll, like, *do it* with you in exchange for math help, don't you?" Her cheeks—her perfect cheeks—pinked up like two bowls of strawberry ice cream.

The phrase *sleep with me* just hanging there in the air made *me* blush. I could feel it. And here is the truth. I *did* and I *do* want to sleep with Alice. How could I say no to that question? I'm almost seventeen years old, and despite my mostly contented loner status and my social inadequacies I have carnal desires that I am all too familiar with, so yes, I want to sleep with Alice Franklin. I want to take her in my arms and kiss her neck just under her hairline and slip my hands under her black T-shirt and touch her skin, which I am sure will be soft and warm and sweet. I want to feel her body under mine in some dark, secret room where no one can bother us. Yes, oh my God, yes, do I want to sleep with Alice Franklin.

But not in the way Alice thought in that moment.

Not like that.

Not in exchange for answers to her Algebra II homework.

So I was not completely lying when I said, "No. No, Alice. Not at all. I just want to help you."

I must have seemed somewhat sincere because Alice stopped

frowning. But she still seemed distrustful of my actions. I wasn't sure what to say next, so I just sat there, certain this plan was hopeless. I'd made a total ass of myself.

And then Alice pushed back from the kitchen table, and I was convinced she was about to kick me out, but she just sighed, a big hefty sigh that was almost too big for someone so small. Then she said, "Why are you being so nice to me anyway?"

"Because . . ." I answered. And I thought about the rumors swirling around Alice. The ones I'd surreptitiously gleaned in the hallways and during passing periods before and after classes.

The party. The sexual texts. The abortion.

I thought about the stall on the second floor that I'd heard students talking about, so recently covered in graffiti about Alice Franklin. They're calling it the Slut Stall.

Alice was waiting for an answer to her question about why I was being so nice. Her face was silent, staring steadily at me.

"Because . . ." I said again. "Because . . . I guess I think you deserve it."

The moment I said it I knew it was exactly the right response.

I also knew it was 100 percent true.

Alice didn't kick me out. She looked down at the kitchen floor for a minute, and then she brought her big brown eyes back to look at me.

"Can you help me with one more problem?" she said, opening her book up again.

"With as many as you want," I told her, and I reached for a pencil.

Kelsie

THESE ARE THE THINGS THAT KEEP RUNNING
through my brain even though I don't want them to:

- The Slut Stall.
- Telling people about Alice and the abortion.
- The Really Awful Stuff that happened to me last
  summer.
- Alice and Tommy that night at Elaine's party.
- Tommy Cray in general.
- Alice Franklin in particular.
- Whether or not I deserve to go to hell if there actually
  is a hell for me to go to.

It's like my brain has been working so crazy hard at not
thinking about certain things that I don't really have time to

appreciate the fact that I'm a full-fledged popular girl now. I sit with Elaine and Maggie and all their friends every single day, right in the middle of the noise and the inside jokes and the attention. I hang out at Elaine's house a lot and we gossip about everything. And it's really fun. I would be a huge, ridiculous liar if I told you it isn't fun.

But.

Still.

The other day I noticed Alice talking to Kurt Morelli in the hallway. Elaine and me and some of the other girls were walking by and there they were. Alice was standing there in her gray sweatshirt and jeans, her arms squeezed up tight around her chest with her hands tucked under her armpits. Like she was trying to shrink into nothing. Kurt was acting like he didn't know where to look or put his body, like he was just really uncomfortable being alive. Alice was saying something and Kurt was nodding his head and it was the weirdest image I'd seen in a long time.

"What the hell is that about?" Elaine muttered to me, and not all that quietly either.

"Oh my God," I said, because it was the only thing I could think of.

"I hope *he* doesn't get her pregnant," somebody added, and we all sort of collapsed into each other, giggling. The thought of Kurt and Alice doing it was so hilarious that we had to hold each other up to keep from passing out with laughter.

I don't know if Alice heard what we said or not.

Seeing her talking to Kurt Morelli was totally bizarre. Even though I know the other girls don't feel the same way, there is still a little part of me that sees Alice as this unattainably cool girl in my freshman homeroom on the first day of high school. The kind of girl who swore out loud with total confidence and deemed me worthy of being her friend even though my mom was way too crazy into religion and I didn't know how to put on eyeliner. The kind of girl who acted like getting asked out by a guy was the most boring thing in the whole world because it happened to her, like, every single day.

So seeing Alice talking to the strangest guy in school was really unsettling.

But the truth is, even though there's some of me that can remember what it was like to meet the Incredible Alice Franklin way back in ninth grade, mostly it feels like the real Alice Franklin has moved away. Or turned into a ghost or a different person. Like she's transformed into a gray sweatshirt with legs.

There's another thing on the list of things I try not to think about. And that is that first time Alice hung out at my house. We wandered into my den, and my brain was working overtime trying to think of what to say to sound cool, and she ran her raspberry-colored fingernails over the spines of all my mom's religious books, including *Jesus Calling* and *Power of a Praying Wife*. I remember how my cheeks flared up super hot as she peered at some of the covers. I remember holding my breath as she looked around the room and took in all the Christian stuff on the walls.

"My mom's really intense about the religion thing," I said, "but I'm, um, totally not." I hoped my mother couldn't overhear our conversation from back in the kitchen. Denying your faith in the Lord was the ultimate no-no.

"Oh," said Alice like she hadn't even noticed. "That's cool. I mean, I believe in God and everything. No big deal."

I remember how my shoulders sank ten feet with relief when she said that.

I miss her. I actually miss her. I know I always got jealous of her and I know she lied to me about giving Mark Lopez a blow job and I know that one of the guys she (probably/maybe) slept with at Elaine's party was Tommy Cray. I know that when I'm the most upset about The Really Awful Stuff, I blame her for it even though logically that doesn't make sense . . . I miss her. I miss doodling on magazines and ordering pizza and eating an entire pan of brownies together just because we wanted to. I miss watching corny, crazy musicals like *Cry-Baby* and *The Apple* and singing the songs out loud. I miss asking her questions about what sex is like and having sleepovers and watching her call boys in the middle of the night and do a really bad Chinese accent and ask if they wanted extra egg rolls with their order. And I miss gossiping and texting in class to fight off our boredom.

Kelsie I am so bored in this class I want 2 poke my eyeballs out with hot sticks.

Don't do it your eyes are pretty.

I could walk around with sticks in my eyes where
the eyeballs had been. You could lead me around
and be my helper.

Are U saying I would be your seeing eye dog?

Yes but not a dog. Just a helpful friend.

U are a freak Alice!!!!

I know U R 2!!!!

I miss her and I know it's a totally hypocritical, pathetic thing
to say. Given everything I've done to her and everything I'll
probably still do.

And all just to sit at the good table in the cafeteria.

But it's true. I'd deny it to anyone who asked me straight out,
but most of the time—actually lots of the time—I miss Alice
Franklin.

I guess I don't deserve to. But I do.

Kurt

EVEN THE GODS THEMSELVES MUST HAVE eventually gotten used to being around Aphrodite.

And so it is that after almost two months of meeting twice a week, I'm finally starting to relax a little at Alice's house. Despite her beauty, her appeal, her perfect knees and lips and face, I'm no longer a jumbly mess during our tutoring sessions. I'm not a placid lake of calmness either, mind you. But I can breathe regularly at least.

She always has her math textbook ready and waiting for me on the kitchen table, next to the sharpened pencils and an ice-cold can of Coke. She never drinks anything during our sessions. She just studies me carefully as I work the problems, offer explanations, answer her questions.

Her mother is almost never home. Once I caught a glimpse of her as she walked out of the house during one of my sessions with Alice. She's an older version of her daughter, but with shoulder-length hair and a face that isn't anywhere near as soft and as sweet as Alice's face. She told Alice not to wait up, and she didn't even say hello to me.

I get the sense that Alice is very much on her own.

One evening after a long set of problems, Alice looked at me and said, "How did you get to be so good at this anyway?"

I shrugged my shoulders and told her the truth. "I don't know. It just comes easily to me, I guess. It's not hard at all. But the things that come easily to other people don't come easily to me, so I suppose there is a trade-off."

"What doesn't come easily to you?" Alice said, frowning a little. "You're a straight A student."

"Academics aren't the problem," I told her. "But, for example, talking to people. About the weather or sports or what have you. I can't do that. I'm not good at just talking."

Alice's slight frown turned into a smile.

"Well, aren't we talking now?"

I flushed. "Yes, we are. We're talking about talking."

"Talking about talking," Alice repeated. Her smile grew a little more. My brain grasped at every corner of my head, searching for something to say, but I couldn't find anything.

After a moment of quiet, Alice said, "Should we get back to work?" Maybe she sensed my discomfort.

"Okay," I said, grateful to be able to talk about polynomials again.

Then I got an idea. The holidays were around the corner, and I thought of a gift I wanted to get Alice. I have money to spend. Plenty, actually. My parents had been smart in their financial planning, and I'm well aware that my grandmother has a sizable amount with which to raise me. I could afford to be magnanimous. When I asked my grandmother for the money I'd need to buy the present, she asked me who it was for.

"Alice Franklin," I said. I can't lie to my grandmother.

"Well," my grandmother answered, "you never ask for anything, Kurt. So I suppose if you want to spend a hundred dollars on this gift, that's your choice."

Would Alice think I was trying to purchase her affection? Maybe. But I searched around online and found what I wanted and bought it anyway, hoping for the best possible outcome. Which is to say, I hoped that Alice Franklin would love her present.

I was scheduled to go to Alice's house on a Thursday evening. But I hadn't realized that that particular Thursday was Brandon Fitzsimmons's seventeenth birthday. Rather, it would have been had he lived. And with this birthday, Healy High plummeted into full grieving mode once again. Brandon's locker was covered with balloons in the school colors and girls started crying in class and lessons were suspended so people could talk about their feelings with a grief counselor that the principal brought in specifically for the occasion.

I hadn't seen Alice at all that day, and when I showed up at her house with my gift in hand, she answered the door, and I knew right away she'd been drinking. There was the smell of beer on her breath, her cheeks were red, and her smile was lop-sided and generous. If I wasn't mistaken, her eyes looked as if she'd been crying.

"Hey, Kurt," she said. She sort of slid toward the kitchen where there was no spiral notebook or Algebra II textbook or sharp-ened yellow pencils. There *was* a can of Lone Star beer on the counter. She took a sip from it with her perfect lips.

"It's what my mother drinks. Isn't it gross? But whatever."

"Oh," I said, unsure of what to do or think.

"Do you want one?" Alice asked me.

"Okay," I said.

I took a fresh can from her and leaned in for a sip, and for a moment my mind sped back to the last time I drank beer. To a warm Saturday night at the very beginning of fall. Then my mind slipped to the thing I wanted to tell Alice Franklin.

It was a Saturday night in the very early fall, not long into junior year. I was up late, reading in my bedroom. It was around one in the morning. Sometimes I suffer from insomnia, but I've come to embrace it over the years because it gives me time to stay up and read. And I've discovered I can actually get by with four or five hours of sleep. I'm lucky that way.

I had the window open. In Healy, you could do that. It was a hot Texas night, but my grandmother loves to turn off the air conditioning during the evenings and open the windows instead. She says it's good for a body to breathe the fresh night air. I'm assuming it's also good for the electric bill.

"Kurt, hey. *Kurt!*"

It was a very loud whisper that actually came out louder than simply speaking in a normal tone of voice. I thought perhaps I'd started to drift off and hear things, but then it came at me again, straight through the open window.

"Kurt Morelli, do you hear me?"

I pulled on my sweatpants and headed to the window. Across the way I saw Brandon Fitzsimmons balancing himself on the roof of his house, just outside his bedroom. He was drinking a can of beer and calling my name.

I put my finger to my mouth to shush him and ventured downstairs, creeping as quietly as I could. When I made it outside, I stared up at Brandon from the ground.

"Morelli," he said, this time not whispering but sort of burping in the middle of uttering my last name. He was drunk. Obviously.

"Fitzsimmons," I answered. "Knackered again, I see."

"If *knackered* is smart boy talk for lit to the tits, then yeah, I am. Morelli, what I love about you is you always shoot straight with me. You don't beat around the bush. You see I'm drunk and you tell me I'm drunk. You see the light of the moon shining down upon you, and you say hi to the moon."

"I haven't said hi to the moon. You're simply incredibly in-toxicated."

"Come up man, just come up."

I shrugged my shoulders and headed toward the back of the Fitzsimmonses' house to get the ladder they keep next to the garage. Starting in the eighth or ninth grade, Brandon had had me up on the roof a few times in the late night hours, so I knew where it was. I laughed to myself as I imagined the rest of the Healy High population catching a glimpse of the highest- and lowest-ranked men in the Healy High hierarchy sitting next to one another on a roof, talking. At school, Brandon didn't ac-knowledge me unless it was to make fun of my size or my grades. Truthfully, he did it so good-naturedly I couldn't really mind. I mean, he called me a poindexter and he grinned when he did it. It was almost quaint.

"Wanna beer?" He slipped his hand inside his bedroom win-dow and handed me one. I opened it.

"Wow, Morelli, I didn't know you had it in you."

"It's beer, not cyanide."

"What's cyanide?"

"A poison. Members of the Jonestown cult consumed it in mass quantities on the order of their leader, Jim Jones. They all died immediately after."

"*Jesus*, Morelli, where do you get this crap?" Brandon said, taking a sip and grinning.

I smiled to myself with satisfaction. Ever since we'd been

young children, Brandon had enjoyed exploring my collection of unusual facts and figures. He would always remind me of that time when we were quite young and I convinced his mother that the roof was structurally sound enough to play on by explaining to her the concept of compressive strength. I could tell he was impressed with my intelligence even if he never admitted it out loud.

Now, despite our occasional nighttime conversations and Brandon's interest in the inner workings of my brain, Brandon wasn't my secret friend or any such nonsense. I knew this, even at the time. He was my neighbor, a person who had been in my life since kindergarten. He was Brandon Fitzsimmons, and I was Kurt Morelli, and for reasons I'm not certain of but could speculate on, he enjoyed talking to me. Perhaps because there was no one else he felt he could tell his secrets and stories to. Perhaps because I humored him. Perhaps because I lived next door.

And I suppose, on some level, I enjoyed speaking to him. Or at least listening to what he had to tell me.

So we talked.

Why did I enjoy listening to him? Brandon was so incredibly different from me in almost every possible way—except for the fact that we were both males living in Healy—that it was almost like anthropological research sitting on the roof next to him, listening to him tell me about his exploits and his adventures and his problems. It provided me insight into a radically different kind of life. I believe I may be the only person in the town who knows that once during a big game he wet his pants out of anxiety. And that the Geometry teacher passed him even though he turned in every single test and quiz completely blank because his status as Healy High quarterback was simply that important. Or that he often forgot the difference between his right and his left. (One night I showed him a trick to help him remember—that his left hand made the shape of a letter *L*—and for this he was quite grateful.)

And so I admit to having enjoyed these evenings. Evenings like that fall night with Brandon drunk and me just drinking. And I was enjoying that particular evening so much that I even started a second beer.

"So where were you this fine Saturday night?" I asked after listening to Brandon complain about how tired he was from that afternoon's game and how much of a blowhard Coach Hendricks could be at times.

"Hanging out at the Healy High parking lot. It was incredible. Just amazing." He was being sarcastic, I realized.

"Being fawned over by your adoring public?"

"I don't understand what you're saying, Morelli. Talk slower." He shoved me with his shoulder.

"I mean, were you getting lots of attention from people in the parking lot? Since you are, after all, Brandon Fitzsimmons."

Brandon laughed and sucked down the rest of his beer.

"I suppose this is when I should tell you that it's not all that it's cracked up to be, being the most popular junior in the school, right? That I just want to be understood and shit."

"So, it isn't all it's cracked up to be?" I asked, honestly curious. Brandon slowly nodded his head in the affirmative, and a sad expression spread on his face. Then he suddenly broke up laughing. "No, man," he told me. "It's pretty awesome, I have to say. I know that makes me sound like a dick, but it is. People love me. I can do no wrong. Chicks love me. Dudes want to be me. Except maybe for you."

I thought about the latest rumor just out around the school involving him and the gorgeous Alice Franklin, and I thought otherwise. So, perhaps emboldened by the beer, I said, "Well, what about Alice Franklin? I heard about the two of you and Elaine's party. I wouldn't mind getting to know her, in the Biblical sense."

Brandon didn't say anything for a moment, then shook his head and chuckled just a bit to himself.

"You mean, you'd like to bang Alice?"

"Well, I don't know if I'd use the phrase *bang*, perhaps, but she's quite a foxy young lady."

"Morelli, I think you're buzzed," Brandon said.

"I think I am, too," I said.

It was quiet for a little while on the roof, and then, out of nowhere, Brandon burped loudly. Then he said, "I didn't do her, you know."

I'd almost forgotten for a moment what we'd been talking about. Then I remembered. Alice Franklin.

"You mean," I said, "you . . . did . . . I mean, people are saying—"

"People are saying that I screwed her and then Tommy Cray screwed her. Yeah, man, I know what people are saying because I told them in the first place! Come on, Morelli. Catch up here."

"But you didn't, uh, bang her?"

"Nope," he said. "Didn't. Bang. Alice."

"Did Tommy?"

"Nope. Not him either."

"So why . . . ?" I was confused. At this point, people had already started treating Alice differently at school, in small but obvious ways. Like not sitting with her as often during lunch. Or laughing when she walked into class.

"Morelli, I don't know why the hell I do the things I do sometimes, if you want to know the truth," Brandon said, and he burped again. "I wanted to get with her that night and she wouldn't get with me. Led me on and then told me she didn't want to fool around. Pissed me off. She should be happy to get with me. Most girls are. Take Maggie Daniels, right? She's a little chunky for my taste, but Maggie Daniels would give her left arm to be with me. Of course then I wouldn't want to be with her because she wouldn't have both arms, and I'm not some kind of pervert." Brandon laughed at his own joke, but I didn't.

"Is Alice the first girl to refuse your advances?" I asked, and I felt a bit strange inside, like the house had suddenly tilted a bit.

"Yup," Brandon said. "That's the truth. I never had a girl say no before. And it made me angry. So I said I did her and Tommy did, too. Sort of to get her to see that she shouldn't have said no."

"But what about Tommy?" I asked.

"I knew Tommy would be going back to college," Brandon answered. "He wouldn't be around to deny it."

I thought of how to explain to Brandon in a way he would understand. "But she's getting so much . . . *shit* for this. You're aware of that, right? I mean, everyone thinks this is true."

Brandon rolled his eyes. "Elaine O'Dea and her whole crew, spreading it around to everyone in creation. But it'll pass. This stuff always does. Give it a week or a month and everyone will forget about it."

I simply could not believe what I was hearing. Never did I think Brandon would have lied about something like that. But he had lied. And what was more, I could tell this utterance on the roof wasn't meant as some revelation or even an admission of guilt. I don't think that Brandon had that level of depth. In his mind, he was merely entertaining me as he usually did with stories about what it was like to be Brandon Fitzsimmons.

We finished our beers wordlessly, and then Brandon said he needed to go to bed.

"Morelli, you're not going to tell anyone about our little secret, right?" he asked, turning around to slide into his room. "I have a reputation to uphold, you know." When he said this, he put his hand on his chest like he was saying the pledge and grinned at me widely.

"Who would I tell?" I answered.

That was the last time I saw Brandon Fitzsimmons alive. The next afternoon as I was helping my grandmother weed her garden, we saw Officer Daniels pull up in front of our house in his official Healy Police Department vehicle.

"Hello, Paul," my grandmother called to him.

"Hello, Vivian," Officer Daniels said, his face looking drawn and pale. Then he told her he needed to speak to her privately, so she left me in the bed of weeds and walked down the driveway to talk to him.

Whatever he told her, my grandmother put her hand up to her mouth and shook her head upon hearing it. I thought it must be news about one of grandmother's church friends, but then I saw her nodding her head yes, and she followed Officer Daniels toward the Fitzsimmonses' house.

"Kurt, give me a moment, please," she said, and I think she was trying not to cry. I watched, confused, as she and Officer Daniels knocked on the door and Mrs. Fitzsimmons let them in. A few moments later, I heard Mrs. Fitzsimmons screaming like an animal at the top of her lungs.

I couldn't tell Alice my story that night. Not like that. Not with Alice buzzed from drinking and her eyes red from possibly crying. So I said nothing.

"I left my math books at school," Alice said, tossing her empty beer can away and opening the refrigerator to find a full one. "So I guess you can't tutor me tonight."

"Okay," I said. It seemed to be the one word I could utter.

We were just standing there in the kitchen. Alice was wearing those dark blue jeans and her shirt was green and loose and draped over her small frame almost like a blanket. She didn't have on any shoes, and her tiny toenails matched the color of her lips. These are the things I notice about Alice Franklin. These are the things I am constantly noticing about Alice Franklin.

"Follow me to the living room, please, my tutor friend," Alice said, and she took one finger and sort of dragged it across my chest as she left the kitchen.

My chest was on fire from Alice's fingertip, and I walked behind her to the living room. It's not a particularly unique living room. It has a window that faces the street, two broken-in beige couches, a few end tables, a television (not the latest model), and a dark blue throw rug in the center of it all.

Alice sat down on one end of one couch, and I sat down on the other end. I drank my beer slowly, and then I asked the only question I could come up with.

"So why aren't we working on math?"

Alice's eyebrows popped up like she was thinking about my question very hard. Then she sighed one of her big loud sighs again and took another sip of beer, and she got a sort of faraway look in her eyes.

And then a few tears started to run down her face.

Soon, she was no longer entertaining a few tears; she was

sobbing. Hard. Hard enough that she got up to grab some paper towels from the kitchen as I sat on the couch, mute and useless.

In all of my Alice Franklin fantasies, sitting on the couch in her house while she cried was not one of them. Something told me I should go to her. Pat her hand. Tell her it was going to be all right. But I couldn't figure out how to make myself do any of those things. And anyway, who could say it was going to be all right? Considering all that Alice Franklin had suffered in recent months, that sort of prediction would be considered highly suspect by anyone in Healy. Most especially Alice.

I almost asked her if I should leave, but I didn't want to leave. I wanted to do the right thing. I clenched a fist in frustration. Why couldn't I just say something? The right thing? Whatever that right thing might be?

"Alice, I have a Christmas present for you."

Alice was back on the couch now, rubbing at her face with a wadded-up paper towel. When she heard what I said, she kept sniffling but her crying slowed down.

"What?" she said, confused.

"Here," I said, walking over to the front door where I'd left my gift, wrapped in some burnished red wrapping paper my grandmother gave me. "This is for you. For Christmas." I handed it to her and then sat back down.

"Oh, Kurt," Alice said, balling up the paper towel before putting it on the coffee table in front of us that was stacked with magazines and remote controls. She was still sniffling, but at least she was no longer sobbing. At least my move worked.

Although I couldn't say it came from any sort of rational plan. My offer of her present was simply the first thing that slipped out of my mouth.

But here was Alice Franklin opening my present, here she was slipping a delicate finger underneath a piece of carefully placed Scotch tape, here she was pulling out the book that cost me more money than I've ever spent in my life at one time.

"Oh, this is my favorite book ever!" Alice said, turning it over in her hands. "How did you know?"

Oh.

This was definitely not part of any rational plan. Despite my alleged intellectual prowess, I hadn't thought this far ahead. How could I tell Alice that I knew *The Outsiders* was her favorite book without admitting to her that I'd been observing almost everything about her since we were in the seventh grade?

"I think you . . . mentioned it once. In an English class we had together."

Alice exhaled one last little shaky, post-crying exhale and seemed to accept this answer. Thank goodness. She opened the book and flipped the pages.

"I've never seen this version of the cover before. Is this . . . old?"

"It's a first edition," I said.

I could see from Alice's face that she didn't know what this meant, but she smiled at me anyway.

Now I have to confess something that may come off as sounding snobbish. In all of my fantasies about Alice Franklin, she knows what a first edition is. And in all of my fantasies about Alice Franklin, not only does she understand this, she understands all of my strange, obscure cultural and historical references and she can even engage with me in long conversations about quantum mechanics.

This is because my fantasy Alice Franklin is perfect.

But that night something occurred to me. I'd never been to fantasy Alice's house. Fantasy Alice had never given me cold Cokes or smiled wide enough to show off her crooked tooth. (Let's face it, Fantasy Alice doesn't even have a crooked tooth.) And I'd never been able to make Fantasy Alice stop crying with a present I'd purchased.

"A first edition is from the first print run," I explained, and I obeyed the brave part of me inside that encouraged me to slide over to Alice's side of the couch and flip the book open to the first few pages. I ran a finger under the copyright date. "See, the very first time the publishing house printed a big bunch of *The Outsiders*, this was one of those books. Before anyone knew how famous it would become or how special it would be." I wanted to add that a first edition of such a famous book is pretty rare, but I didn't want to sound stuck up about everything. And anyway, you could tell from Alice's facial expression that she understood the precious quality of this book in her hands, and I don't mean financially.

She smiled broadly and closed the book and opened it again. Then she bent her head down and smelled the pages.

"It smells good," she said to me. "Very first edition."

I grinned back at her. It felt quite good to grin with Alice Franklin.

"I hope you like it," I said.

"Oh, Kurt. I love it. But I didn't get you anything. You're helping me. I should have bought you something. You gave me a first edition of *The Outsiders* and all I gave you was one of my mom's shitty beers."

"It's okay," I said. "This beer is not so shitty."

"Oh, God, yes it is. No, I'm going to order us a pizza," Alice said. "A Christmas pizza."

She wouldn't let me pay, and soon we were sharing a pizza with green peppers and pepperoni.

"This is a very festive meal, Alice," I told her, aware of my sudden ability to talk to her. Maybe it was the Lone Star. I admit that for one second it was awkward to eat in front of such a beautiful girl, but Alice is a messy eater, I noticed. She licked her fingers and took big bites. Watching her gorgeous raspberry lips open and close over and over made me slightly dizzy if I looked at them too long, but more than anything else, I just enjoyed sitting in the living room, drinking Lone Star beer and eating Christmas pizza with Alice Franklin.

Not the fantasy version, but the real thing.

Kelsie

ONCE WHEN I WAS HELPING MY MOM CLEAR out some boxes in our attic back in Flint, I found a shoebox full of photographs of her and my dad. I pulled one photo out of the box and stared at it. The people in the picture looked completely different from the parents I have now, and that's because they were. My mom had a nose ring and a streak of pink hair. My dad had a beard and a knit hat that looked filthy, and he was wearing a T-shirt that said "The Melvins."

"Chicago, 1993" was scrawled on the back in blue ink.

That was before Jesus became my mom's BFF. Three years before she got pregnant with me, back when they were living together (and not married!).

"Mom, who were the Melvins?" I asked, handing her the photograph.

My mom took it out of my hands. My mom with the normal

mom hair and ironed khaki slacks and little gold cross hanging around her neck. For the briefest, teeniest, tiniest second I think she smiled, but then it was like she'd been caught doing something illegal because she shoved the picture inside the shoebox and pushed the box into a pile she'd designated for the trash.

"Just a band," she said, her smile gone. "From back in the bad old days."

Mom used to tell me all the time that I was the reason she rediscovered Jesus and was saved from a life of sin. From the time I was little, she'd told me how surprised she'd been when she'd turned up pregnant with me, and how she'd moved back home to Flint after my dad said he wasn't sure if he wanted to have a kid at nineteen. But then, after my mom started going to church with my grandparents and started praying really hard for Jesus to come into her life again or whatever, my dad had a change of heart and followed her to Flint and they got married and one month later I was born.

"Jesus worked on Dad's heart and my heart, and it's all thanks to you, Kelsie," my mom would say to me. I wondered—if that were true—why my dad sometimes fell asleep during church and argued with my mom about whether or not God wanted him to have that third Miller Lite. But when my mom told me this as a little kid, it made me feel special. This was back when I was pretty sure God loved me. Back before The Really Awful Stuff.

The Really Awful Stuff happened the summer Alice was working at Healy Pool North, and it involved Tommy Cray. It was
the summer of Mark Lopez and the blow job and Alice lying to
me and then telling me I could never possibly understand because I was a virgin.

But before I explain what happened, what has to be said is
that Tommy Cray was and is gorgeous. He's got this permanent
smirk that looks more handsome than mean, muscles that are
obvious but not too overwhelming, and gorgeous calves with
the lightest blond hair on them, so light you can barely see it.
Back then, that summer before tenth grade, I could have stared
at his calves all day. I think it's fair to say he's way more gorgeous than Brandon Fitzsimmons ever was, if you ask me.

Whenever I'd bike down to Healy Pool North to hang out
with Alice, all I'd think about on the ride there was how I was
going to get to watch Tommy Cray. The way he walked, the way
he chewed gum, the way he twirled his lifeguard whistle around
his finger three times to the right and then three times to the
left. I tried really hard to make it look like I wasn't trying too
hard to catch a glimpse of him, but I knew Tommy Cray could
tell how much I liked him anyway. It was like I was drunk or on
drugs or something that summer. I couldn't stop thinking about
Tommy every millisecond that I was awake, and sometimes I
thought about him when I was asleep, too.

"Hey, Kelsie," he'd say, grinning at me when he saw me
working on my tan or heading toward the snack bar to say hi to
Alice.

"Hey, Tommy," I'd answer back, acting like I was just walking by, like I hadn't even known he'd be working that afternoon. I'd imagine he was staring at my butt as I left wet footprints on the cement. But I never turned around to make sure.

One afternoon toward the end of the summer, a few days after Alice had admitted to me that she'd lied about giving Mark Lopez that blow job, I was hanging out by myself at the pool, reading *Seventeen*. Even though I was still kind of mad at Alice for lying to me, I was texting her and trying to get her to come down to see me even though she wasn't scheduled to work, so she could keep me company as I stalked Tommy.

And then, all of a sudden, the most miraculous thing happened.

Actually, it was the worst thing ever as I came to realize later on.

But in the moment, it was miraculous.

"You wanna go for a ride?"

I looked up and there was Tommy standing over me, wearing a Healy Pool North T-shirt and red board shorts. His blond hair had gotten even blonder over the past couple of weeks, and I knew that behind his Ray-Bans his blue eyes probably looked even bluer.

I was being asked by Tommy Cray if I wanted to go for a ride. Even though I couldn't really talk to boys very well, here one stood before me. The one I wanted. And he was talking to *me*.

Somehow, on that steamy August afternoon, I managed to open my mouth and say, "Uh, now?"

"Yeah, now," Tommy Cray said. "Why not?"

"Okay, sure," I said, trying to act like boys were always asking me to go for rides. My heart was beating so strongly it was like my entire body was pulsating on the pink-and-white lounge chair.

A few minutes later we were eating Sonic hamburgers in his used Toyota, and when I got ketchup on my chin, Tommy reached over with one finger and scooped it off, then licked it off his finger. I thought I might get sick from nervousness, sitting there in that car with Tommy Cray. He did most of the talking. How he was leaving for college in a few days, how he had to pack all his stuff, how he wasn't sure if he was going to like his roommate or not.

"Well, we'll all miss you around here," I said. Oh my God, how stupid I sounded. Like a total nerd.

But Tommy Cray just smiled at me.

Then he asked me, "You wanna come over and hang out at my house for a while?"

"Yeah, sure," I said, my head all swimmy and dizzy.

It was the middle of the day and there was no one home. As I followed him inside, I think I knew what was going to happen even before it happened. My whole body felt electric, numb. I heard Alice's words marching through my head: *Kelsie, it's just . . . you know . . . you haven't, like . . . been with anyone . . . in that way. And that's . . . fine, okay? But . . . it's just, like . . . once you've had sex . . . I mean . . ."*

I was scared and excited at the same time. Right then I knew. I was going to lose my virginity to Tommy Cray.

Now don't get me wrong. I'm not stupid. I don't think I ever thought that by sleeping with Tommy I would make him my boyfriend. Even as I followed him to his bedroom wordlessly, even as I let him peel off my cover-up and untie my bikini top before we'd even shut the bedroom door, even as all of this was happening to me, I knew that Tommy Cray would be gone in a few days. I knew he would soon be meeting gorgeous college girls who would want to mess around with him immediately. I knew that he thought I was a Stalker Girl. Easy access. I knew all of this, but it was like I had to do it. That had been the whole point of the entire afternoon. Maybe even the entire summer.

Tommy Cray had a huge poster of Jimi Hendrix on one wall of his bedroom. It was bright yellow and purple and in a loopy, trippy font it said "Are You Experienced?"

Well, Kelsie—are you?

I wasn't, but Tommy Cray was. He leaned into me, the chlorine scent of his skin slipping over my body.

"Kelsie, you're so beautiful," he said. "I've noticed you all summer long."

I just smiled back and nodded, unable to talk. I tried to memorize everything about that moment. The way the hair on his chest was so fine and blond and curled just so, just like the hair on his magnificent calves. The way his lips tasted like Sonic and vanilla Carmex. The way he put his hands on me wherever he wanted to, and I let him.

I'm doing it. I'm actually doing it. Right now at this moment I'm doing it.

It hurt. Like hell. And it was over in three minutes.

Afterward, all I wanted to do was put on my clothes. It had all happened so fast that my bathing suit was still damp from swimming in the pool that afternoon. I yanked my cover-up over me and sat up on the bed, not sure what to say. Tommy reached over and grabbed his shorts. The little whisper in the back of my head that reminded me we hadn't used protection got louder all of a sudden, but I told it to shut up. Tommy hadn't mentioned using anything, and I guess I just followed his lead.

"You didn't tell me," he said.

It hurt between my legs. Ached, actually.

"I didn't tell you what?" I asked. His room was a mess, I noticed suddenly. Even though he was leaving for school soon, he hadn't packed a thing, apparently. A sandwich that looked about five days old was sitting on his desk. I was pretty sure it was growing mold.

"That you'd never done it before." He wasn't looking at me. It was like he thought I was going to freak out. I think at that moment I wanted to, but I knew I wouldn't ever let myself freak out in front of him.

"So what?" I said like it was no big deal. "Everyone has to

have a first time at some point." I wondered how he could tell. I guessed whatever I was supposed to have done, I didn't do correctly.

No, I wasn't experienced. Not at all.

Tommy Cray picked at a mosquito bite on his ankle, and then I caught him glancing at the clock radio by his bed. I saved myself some embarrassment and said, "I should be getting home."

"'Kay," he said. He seemed relieved.

We'd hardly even kissed.

I told Tommy to drop me off a block from my house so my mother wouldn't see his car.

He leaned over and gave me a quick peck before I got out of the Toyota.

"Well, good luck at school," I said. I was desperate for him to say something sweet or romantic. Something to make me feel like maybe it had all been worth it.

"Thanks," he said. "You should text me sometime."

"Cool," I said, and I got out of the car and walked home. Halfway there I realized I didn't even know his number.

I didn't tell Alice. I know. Half the reason I probably even did it with Tommy was because there was this weird little part of me that wanted to prove to her that I wasn't some inexperienced virgin. Of course, after I did it with Tommy, I mostly felt like an inexperienced *non*virgin, so I wasn't sure much had changed.

But the thought of telling Alice that I had slept with a guy who wasn't even my boyfriend—just a guy who'd picked me up at the *pool* for God's sake—was just too weird. Too embarrassing. Sure, Alice had fooled around with Mark Lopez under similar circumstances, but she hadn't slept with him.

For days after it happened, I kept waiting for Tommy to call me or text me, and I kept walking around the house those last few moments of summer, staring at myself in mirrors and thinking, "I'm not a virgin anymore."

He never texted me or called me.

But that's not The Really Awful Stuff.

Not even close.

So what do you think happens to the girl from the Christian family who only does it once? Do I actually have to spell it out for you?

By the time I found out I was pregnant, Tommy Cray was a freshman at Texas Tech and I was a month and a half into my sophomore year at Healy High. Everyone was focused on the start of school, on who they were going to take to the first Fall Dance, on the likelihood of the Healy Tigers taking state . . . and I was trying not to throw up in my breakfast cereal every day.

It can't be, I thought to myself. But it was. All those True Love Waits rallies my mother had dragged me to, all those lectures about saving myself for my future husband, all those reminders that Jesus prefers virgins . . . it was like some sort of ridiculous joke. Who gets pregnant from doing it one time?

But the answer was me. Kelsie Sanders.

One Saturday afternoon while my dad was working and my mom was taking my sister shopping for shoes, I walked down to Seller Brothers and stole a pregnancy test. All the cashiers know my entire family, so there was no chance I could buy one. I figured I'd already fornicated, so what was stealing a home pregnancy test going to do to me?

The two blue lines stared up at me like they were proud of themselves. They were so blue. There was no doubt in their existence. They were just there, proving the worst possible thing in the world.

I was going to have a baby.

I told nobody. Nobody. When I did it with Tommy Cray, my entire body went numb. But this was like my body didn't even exist anymore. It was just my brain and those two blue lines. I was a zombie. I wrapped the pregnancy test in some toilet paper and hid it in the drawer of my nightstand. I stared at myself in the bathroom mirror just like I'd done after doing it with Tommy. I stared at my dark brown hair and my even darker brown eyes. At the freckles on my nose. At the gap between my front teeth.

I was going to have a baby.

I mean, I had to. There was nothing else that I could even picture happening. Ever since I'd been a kid, my mom had been dragging me to the Women's Care Clinic and Planned

Parenthood on Saturday mornings and making me hold up pictures of aborted fetuses. Ever since I was a kid, I'd been told to pray for the souls of the preborn. Ever since I was a kid, I'd been taught that having an abortion is pretty much basically the worst possible thing that any woman could ever do ever. *Ever.*

After all, wasn't I, Kelsie Sanders, proof of the power of Choosing Life? Hadn't I, Kelsie Sanders, been an unplanned pregnancy? A surprise from God, as my mother liked to put it? A surprise that got her to dye her hair back to a normal color and leave Chicago and stop listening to bands with weird names?

So now it was my turn. Only I hadn't even had a chance to get my nose pierced.

But I was going to have a baby anyway.

It was like trying to picture myself making dinner on Mars or speaking fluent Chinese. It was impossible, but it was the only option.

I thought about living in my parents' house for the rest of my life. Me and the baby. Me and the baby in the wood-paneled den and me and the baby in the kitchen with the refrigerator that never stops humming and me and the baby in my teeny pink bedroom in the middle of the night, staring out the window at the stars and planning our escape.

All I could think was, I'm sorry, baby.

So, abortion was out of the question, and I wasn't going to be one of those girls who can hide her pregnancy under a sweater for nine months and then give birth at the prom. So I did what I had to do. I told my mother. She made me take three tests in front of her. I literally had to pee in front of my mother. In between tests I took big swallows from a can of Diet Coke balancing on the bathroom sink. After each test my mother grabbed the stick from my hands, and I think some of my pee actually got on her at one point. She didn't seem to care. She just reached down between my legs and took the test and stared at it, and then she ripped open another package.

"All right," she said to me. She was weirdly calm. My mom was just never that calm. She quotes Jesus constantly and everything, but even having the love of the Lord inside of her hasn't made her very relaxed. She still manages to snap at me constantly and criticize me all the time and get all tense with my dad, and even if she does stop to close her eyes and quote some Bible verse, my mom just isn't a naturally calm person.

Until I turned up pregnant.

"All right, Kelsie, I will take care of this," my mother said, and all of a sudden I thought I was going to have to give this baby up for adoption. I put my arms around my stomach when I thought about it. I'm not going to sit here and lie and tell you I felt instant love for that baby. Mostly, I just felt sick all the time and so tired I could barely stay up past seven o'clock. I thought about handing the baby over to some nice couple from Louisiana or whatever, and it didn't seem so bad. Maybe they'd send me Christmas pictures and let me come to his first birthday party. Maybe they'd let him have a dog, unlike my mother who thinks that animals in the house just make a gigantic mess.

I promised myself that if I got to choose the adoptive parents, I'd make *sure* they'd let him have a dog.

About a week after I took the tests, my mother woke me up at five in the morning on a Saturday. I didn't know what was going on.

"Get dressed, Kelsie," she said to me, whispering. She was dressed in jeans and a black T-shirt. She wasn't wearing any makeup, which was weird because my mom always wears makeup. And she almost always wears skirts and dresses and khaki slacks, not jeans.

"What's going on?" I said. As soon as I sat up, a wave of nausea ran through me. I pressed my hands down on either side of my body, trying to steady myself, and I took a deep breath.

"Get dressed," she said again, standing there next to my bed.

My dad and sister must have still been asleep. I pulled on some clothes and followed her out to the car. I kept asking her what was going on, but she just told me to hurry up. Usually, I don't mind talking back to my mom no matter how many Bible verses she says I'm disobeying, but this morning my mom was being so weird, I was scared to say anything.

We pulled out onto the highway and headed for the city.

"Kelsie, we're going to take care of things," she said, staring out the windshield, not looking at me. I glanced at her face once in a while and then I looked out at the billboards and the run-down houses that popped up on the sides of the highway. It was still dark, but the sun was just starting to come up. I think that was the moment I knew what my mom was planning, but I couldn't believe it could possibly be true.

There in the car that morning when I glanced at my mom's neutral expression, I kept thinking back to that picture I'd found in the attic back in Flint. The funny-colored hair. The nose ring. The look on her face that told me—even if she'd never admit it—that back then, she'd been having fun. Lots of it. I knew I could stare at my mother's face for the rest of her life, and I'd never see that same expression on it ever again. She'd left it back in Chicago in 1993.

She kept on driving.

All the times I'd seen the Women's Care Clinic, it had been from the outside. It's big and gray and the windows are small, skinny strips of glass that are so tiny they might as well not even exist. It looked like a prison. I'd felt really bad every single time we protested there, if you want to know the truth. Even though deep down inside I was pretty sure that abortion must be murder (after all, what else could it be if it isn't that?), when I looked at the faces of the girls and the women walking in for an appointment and how sad and confused they looked, I didn't see the point of all the protesting. What is it ever really going to change? Sometimes I'd seen girls that looked my age walking inside, and they'd be holding on to women who had to be their moms, and the girls would sort of lean their heads in and cry against their moms' shoulders as they walked past us. The couple of times I'd seen a mother-daughter pair like that, I'd been a little jealous. Me. Jealous of a girl getting an abortion because she gets to cry on her mom's shoulder.

So that should tell you something.

When we went into the clinic, it was so early there weren't any protestors outside yelling at us yet, and I knew my mom had planned it this way. I didn't get to cry on my mom's shoulder. Not that she would've let me if I had tried. She just walked me into the lobby and we got frisked by a security guard who looked like he weighed about five hundred pounds. Then we got buzzed into another room, and from that moment on it's just this weird blur in my mind.

My mom never actually said, "Kelsie, you're going to have an abortion." Later on, I figured out my mom probably believed not saying it makes it like it never happened. Because after that day, she never talked about it again. Like that day just never even happened.

I knew the clinic people must have recognized us, but they acted like they didn't, and for that I was really thankful. I sat in the waiting room and I stared at my sneakers, and I tried to figure out how I felt. Relieved? Scared? Sad? Really, I don't know what I felt. I didn't have time *to* feel.

My mom filled out some forms and she didn't talk to me once. I overheard her confirming with the nurse that we lived at least one hundred miles away from the clinic, so we could have the procedure completed in just one trip. Soon I was in a room with just a nurse and a doctor, and I was holding the nurse's hand, and the nurse was so nice. She was, like, ridiculously nice. She kept explaining everything that was going to happen step by step by step, and the entire time she never let go of my hand. Her hand was so warm and soft, it was like wrapping my hand up in a cotton T-shirt straight from the dryer.

"You're so nice," I said to her. "Thank you for being so nice." Hot tears were sneaking out, and I tried to blink them back, but I couldn't, so they just ran out of my eyes and down my cheeks.

"Of course, sweetheart," the nurse said, and she leaned into me, crinkling my blue paper gown. She pressed up against my shoulder and I smelled her skin, which smelled like talcum powder. She was wearing a thin chain with a tiny cross around her neck just like my mother's. Her purple scrubs were covered in butterflies.

"Thank you for being so nice," I said again, and I said this over and over during the whole entire thing. If I could keep on saying it, it would make everything okay. I was convinced of that.

"Of course, sweetheart," the nurse said every single time, and her voice was so gentle, so soft. She kept answering me even as she stopped to tell me what was happening, step by step by step.

Thank you for being so nice.

Thank you for being so nice.

On the drive home I didn't feel well. I guess she knew I might get sick, because my mother had come prepared with a plastic bag from Seller Brothers in the front seat, and she gave it to me when I told her I felt like throwing up.

"Can't we pull over?" I asked her when I saw what she was handing me.

"No," my mother said, never taking her eyes off the road. "Use the bag."

I've made my mom look pretty evil, but I guess when we got home she wasn't so bad. She helped me into bed, and she sat on the edge of the mattress reading the aftercare instructions on the paper the clinic gave her. She studied them like she was going to be quizzed on them later or something. I'm not sure what she told my dad or sister, but no one except for my mom came into my bedroom for the rest of the weekend. I just sat in my bed looking through magazines and ignoring all of Alice's texts and calls and thinking about the nurse at the clinic and how I wished she could come and sit with me for a while and hold my hand.

Like I said, my mom and I never talked about The Really Awful Stuff again. Ever. She never even asked who got me pregnant. The only thing that changed was she stopped making me go to protests with her at the Women's Care Clinic. She still goes though. I wonder what the clinic people think when they see her out there.

For a while after it all happened, for like a couple of weeks or so, I kept thinking I was still pregnant. I would wake up to the buzzing of my alarm, and for a second I'd think, "Oh my God, I'm pregnant." Then I would remember that I wasn't anymore. I kept waiting to feel something. Relief or sadness or anything. But mostly I just felt nothing. I didn't tell anyone anything, either. Not even Alice. A couple of times I almost did, but just as I was about to open my mouth, the thought of going through everything all over again just seemed totally exhausting.

I'm a pretty good actress, though, because I wasn't half bad at just going through the sophomore year motions and getting decent grades and being semi-popular and whatever. I could still gossip with Alice and I could still laugh at everything the cool girls said and I went to parties and drank and rolled my eyes at the stupid jokes the boys made, and in general I tried not to think about anything.

I saw Tommy Cray again. Of course I did. It's Healy. You see everyone again. It was Christmas break of tenth grade, and I would have been like five months along if what happened hadn't happened. Even though it eventually sank into my head that I wasn't pregnant anymore, sometimes if no one was around I would get on the computer and read about what the baby would have been like: Your baby has eyebrows. Your baby will get startled at loud noises. You can feel your baby moving.

Right around when I saw Tommy Cray, the baby would have been the size of a banana. I would have started to feel him move. Tommy's family was eating dinner at The Hot Biscuit and my family was eating there, too, and I saw him from across the dining room, and I just couldn't eat. My dad was getting all upset because it's not like we can afford to go out to eat all the time, and my little sister was all, "I'll eat her share," because she hates fights, especially fights between me and my parents. I was getting ready for my mom to say something about Jesus not liking us to waste good food when Tommy's family got up to leave.

"I'll be right back," I said, and I just stood up without waiting to be excused and walked across the room, heading right for Tommy.

"Kelsie?" Tommy said when he saw me, surprised.

"Can I talk to you a sec?" I said, totally ignoring the fact that we were in the middle of The Hot Biscuit and his mom and dad and brothers were staring at me wondering what the heck I was doing.

"Uh, now?" he said. "We're getting ready to leave."

"It's really important," I said, and I didn't turn around to see if my family was looking at me.

"Tommy, we're waiting outside," Mrs. Cray said, looking confused but still trying to seem polite. She was wearing one of those hideous Christmas sweaters most people only wear as a joke, but I got the feeling she was serious about it. I felt like yelling out, "You were almost a grandma!" Maybe I was losing my mind.

Tommy and I moved toward the waiting area of The Hot Biscuit, right near "The Hostess Will Seat You" sign.

"So what's up?" he said. I hadn't seen him or talked to him since we did it. It was so weird.

"I just wanted you to know," I said, lowering my voice to a whisper, "that I got pregnant." I can't believe I admitted it there, like, right in the middle of The Hot Biscuit. But I guess in a way it was a relief that there was finally someone I could say that to out loud. Finally I wasn't just saying it to myself in my own head.

Tommy's eyes opened really big and he glanced down at my stomach, which was as flat as a pancake, of course.

"What?" he said, all confused.

"I'm not pregnant *now*," I told him, hoping he would figure it out.

"Um," Tommy said, scratching the back of his neck. "Can I, like, call you tonight? I really can't do this right now."

"Okay, but you'd better actually call me," I said, shocking even myself as I slowly gave Tommy my number and he punched it into his phone.

When I got back to our table, no one said anything about why I got up. I acted like I just went to the bathroom. My mom looked at me and then glanced toward the front door where Tommy had just walked out. Maybe she put it together and maybe she didn't. Who knows?

"How's your meal?" our waitress asked, coming over.

"Everything's just lovely," my mother said, giving her a smile only I knew was fake.

This is shocking, but Tommy actually did call me. Late, after 10:00 p.m., but he called. At first he did all that stuff, like are you sure it was mine, but we only did it once, and blah blah blah. I guess the fact that I wasn't still pregnant made it less scary for him to talk about it with me. My brain kept going back to that summer afternoon in his messy bedroom and the moldy sandwich and the Jimi Hendrix poster.

Three minutes in that room and everything changed forever.

"Man, Kelsie, I'm sorry," Tommy said, and I think maybe he actually was a little. "I can't believe it."

"Why didn't you use anything?" I asked, digging my fingernails into my palm, working up the nerve it took to ask that question.

"I don't know," he said. "I guess I thought since you didn't say anything, you were on the Pill or something."

"Oh," I said. "Well, I wasn't."

"Yeah, well. Obviously."

We didn't say anything for a while because really we had nothing *to* say to each other. We'd made small talk at the pool and had sex once. That was it.

"So how's sophomore year other than that?" Tommy asked, and I wanted to smack him through the phone. I guess he meant it in a friendly way and everything, but come on. How's tenth grade other than your abortion?

"Oh, it's been awesome. It's been totally amazing, actually," I said, my voice tense with sarcasm.

"Come on, Kelsie, I'm just trying to be nice. I'm sorry. I

really am, but I'm not sure exactly what I should be saying here. I mean, it wasn't like you and me were girlfriend and boyfriend," he said.

Somehow, hearing him say that hurt more than I expected it to.

"Yeah, I know," I said, and all of a sudden I just wanted to get off the phone.

"Come on, I didn't mean it like that," Tommy said, and I just said, "Okay," and I hung up on him. I wondered for a second if he was going to try and call me back, but he didn't.

Just before midnight as I was about to go to sleep, he texted me.

**don't be mad we can still be friends I'm sorry about
everything**

Like we were ever friends. Like we were ever anything at all.

Later on, when it first came out about Alice (probably/maybe) sleeping with Tommy and Brandon at the party, I wasn't jealous. Not really. Even as she swore up and down that nothing had happened, all I could think about was how crazy it was that it had been Alice's words that had kind of talked me into sleeping with Tommy in the first place.

And then she went and slept with him, too. I mean probably. Maybe.

Every time I thought about those words coming out of Alice's mouth—those sort of gentle, pitying words—I thought about walking into Tommy's bedroom that summer afternoon. I thought about the cool dampness of my bathing suit on my suntanned skin, of the softness of the carpet as I slipped off my candy cane–striped flip-flops and sank down onto Tommy's unmade bed, knowing there wasn't any turning back.

I wondered if my life would have been different if maybe Alice Franklin had never said those words to me.

I'd told myself I'd give myself a year to feel sad about The Really Awful Stuff and then I wouldn't think about it anymore. And then so much happened in that one year. Elaine's party. The car accident. Alice getting blamed for Brandon's death. Alice not being my friend anymore.

And then one night, just about a year to the day of that miserable morning at the clinic, I had a dream that I was dancing on our back deck holding a baby boy with blond hair and blue eyes bluer than the water at Healy Pool North. And I had this sick, scary feeling like even though the next day was the deadline for not being sad anymore, just naming a date wasn't going to work.

And then the next day I found myself with Elaine and Maggie and all the other girls in the bathroom. I still felt like I needed to prove to them that I was on their side and not Alice's. Like I really needed them to know I wanted to stay friends with them, not anyone else. And my head kept getting filled up with snatches of that dream of the baby and also little snippets of the

Jimi Hendrix poster and the nice nurse holding my hand and my scary mom and Tommy never calling me and Alice's words. Alice's words.

My head hurt. Elaine looked bored. No one was saying anything. I wondered if it was because I was there. They didn't really like me. They could smell my old middle school nerdiness on me like it was some kind of disease. They were this close to getting rid of me, I just knew it.

So I got all dramatic and said to the other girls, "Okay, so I have to tell you something. About Alice."

Lying about Alice and starting the Slut Stall was something Kelsie from Flint wouldn't have ever done.

So I guess that's why I did it.

JOSH

I HATE SCHOOL. I'M NOT GOOD AT IT AND I don't get the point. I have no idea what I'm going to do once I graduate Healy High, but I can tell you that it sure as hell isn't going to involve Algebra or Chemistry or the Gettysburg Address.

But I still try to do good. I mean, I don't want to end up in summer school. It wasn't so bad when I would go with Brandon. We would sit in the back row and make stupid jokes. But this summer Brandon won't be around to make summer school less painful. He won't be around to make Two-A-Days less painful.

He just won't be around.

The other day I had to research this history paper that was already late, so I went down to the library during study hall to mess around on one of the computers. I have a computer at home and everything, but my brother is always screwing around on it or my mom is on it or whatever, so I figured I would just go down to the Healy High library and do my research there.

I was hoping someone from my class would be in there so we could joke around and make the whole research thing not so painful, even though most kids spend Study Hall in the auditorium where they let you talk. Maybe if there was some girl I knew in the library I could even get her to help me do the work. I'm always looking for someone to help me do the work.

But when I walked into the library, the only person in the whole entire place was Alice Franklin.

I didn't see her when I walked in because she was sort of hidden in the back at a table behind some reference books no one hardly even uses anymore. I just saw her because I was walking around in that part of the library. She had some math homework in front of her.

It was weird because I just turned the corner and there she was. Sitting all alone at this table, her book open and this spiral notebook full of problems. She heard me come up, I guess, because she looked up and there we were, staring at each other.

She looked shocked to see me for a second, but that only lasted for a second. She mostly just stared at me. At first it was like she was just looking me over, and then maybe I think I saw her eyebrows sort of come together a little, like she was mad. But maybe almost like she was scared to get mad.

She knew I'd said she'd been texting Brandon. She knew everyone blamed Brandon's death on her because of me. I mean, I don't know who exactly told her I'd said anything, but it took about twenty seconds for everyone in Healy to find out about that, so it doesn't really matter anyway.

I can't believe I just stood there, looking at Alice like some big dummy. I don't know what my face looked like. Alice took a deep breath and then when it came out it sounded all shaky. Real fast she stood up and slammed her books and held them across her chest and just walked past me. Real quickly, and she didn't look at me either when she walked by.

I stood there for a second watching her go. Then Mrs. Long, the librarian, came up to me.

"Josh, honey, do you need some assistance?"

I nodded yes and told her about the paper, and then I followed her to the computers so she could look stuff up for me. I knew if I smiled and was real sweet, she would really help me out. It's one of the perks of being me, I guess.

As Mrs. Long was typing stuff into one of the databases, my brain remembered this one time in middle school when Alice and me had been assigned to be partners for this autobiography project. By this time I was cool enough not to throw paper wads in her hair anymore, and we were sort of even friends.

"I really want to do our project on Vince Young," I remembered telling her.

"Who is Vince Young?" Alice asked, and she wrinkled up her nose.

"Oh my God, Alice, how do you not know who Vince Young is?" I remembered how I pretended to pass out from the shock, and Alice had laughed that loud funny laugh she has.

But she gave in, and we did do our project on Vince Young. She even did almost all the work anyway and she wasn't even nasty about it.

As Mrs. Long hummed and typed and talked, I just kept remembering that project. I kept thinking about how I made Alice laugh and how nice she had been about the whole thing.

The deal is, I know I'm dumb sometimes, but I try real hard most of the time not to be an asshole. And I guess that day in the library, I just felt like an asshole.

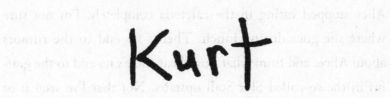

Kurt

SHORTLY AFTER SHARING CHRISTMAS PIZZA
and beer with Alice Franklin, we reached the end of the first
semester at Healy High. It's always a half day before Winter
Break, and there's no real purpose in even going to school that
day. It's merely an excuse to eat candy and watch movies in
class. On most days I feel the work at Healy High is much too
easy for me, but on days like the half day before Winter Break, I
feel insulted that I'm even expected to show up for school.

But I tried to get into the spirit of things. Since I've been tutoring Alice, there's a reason to look forward to walking the
halls of the school building. I might see Alice there, and she'll
smile at me. Dip her head ever so slightly. Peer out from that
sweatshirt and raise her eyebrows at me in a greeting.

I know I'm the only one on the receiving end of those greet-
ings, and this makes me feel special and happy. In fact, I'm

fairly certain that I'm the only one at Healy High who Alice speaks to anymore. Sometimes I have fantasies that she will come and eat lunch with me in the cafeteria, but a few weeks ago, Alice stopped eating in the cafeteria completely. I'm not sure where she goes during lunch. There's no end to the rumors about Alice, and from what I overhear there's no end to the graffiti in the so-called Slut Stall upstairs. Not that I've seen it or want to see it.

On the half day before break there was no lunch served, of course, and my stomach was growling as I prepared to gather my books out of my locker and head home. Maybe I was feeling light-headed from lack of nutrition, because it's the only explanation for the bold act I soon found myself committing.

I found her as I was walking out of the main hallway. She had on that sweatshirt, and her backpack was slung low against her rear end. I tried not to glance there too long because it made me feel a little guilty, honestly. She was alone, staring into the trophy case full of team photographs and rusting trophies from decades past.

"Hello, Alice," I said, standing next to her. I felt like this was something I could do. After all, we ate pizza together. We drank beer together. She cried in front of me. I gave her a Christmas present. We worked together at her house twice a week. But still, I was nervous to discover her reaction.

I shouldn't have been. Alice turned to me and smiled. Smiled broadly enough that her crooked incisor peeked out at me.

"Hello, Kurt," she said, and although I know it's biologically impossible, my heart dropped down into my stomach for a moment before returning to my chest.

"What are you looking at?" I asked, motioning to the trophy case.

"Oh, I guess I'm wondering how many of these people ever left Healy," she said, peering back at some old photos from the seventies, complete with long hair and bell-bottoms.

"Probably not many."

"Probably you're right. So, are you ready for break?"

"I certainly am," I answered. "Are you?"

Alice shook her head ruefully but she smiled. "Do you even have to ask that question?"

We stood there for a moment, and then my food-starved brain made its move.

"Alice, would you like to come over to my house to have lunch? To celebrate the next two weeks without Healy High?"

Alice mastered a response that was the perfect blend of politeness and shock. She smiled and opened her eyes wide at the exact same moment. For that small space of time, it was as if we had been transported back in time. Back to the days before the rumors and the bathroom stall and the banishment. Back to the days when someone like me asking someone like Alice Franklin over to his house for lunch would be akin to successfully confirming the existence of the fourth dimension.

Impossible.

But it was not that time. It was now, and after Alice processed what I was saying, she said, "Okay, sure. Yes. That would be great."

"My grandmother is making grilled cheese sandwiches," I said, and I instantly regretted saying anything so stupid. I sounded like a kindergartner. Alice had been to parties where people smoked marijuana and got drunk. Regardless of the validity of the rumors about her and Brandon Fitzsimmons, Alice Franklin was almost certainly not a virgin, yet here I was, a virgin talking about grilled cheese sandwiches.

"I like grilled cheese sandwiches," she said.

"Well," I told her, "good. But unfortunately, I don't have any shitty Lone Star beer to go with it."

Alice laughed, and I was pleased at myself for coming up with such a reply and pleased she got the reference.

As we walked out of the school, there were groups of students clumped together in front of the main entrance. Some were wearing Santa hats to celebrate the season. Others were texting or playing with their phones. I could feel eyes on us as the two of us strolled past.

"Well, Kurt," she whispered, and her voice sounded even more appealing in a whisper, "how does it feel to be seen walking the streets with the biggest slut at Healy High?"

"Probably the same as you feel walking the streets with the school's biggest weirdo," I answered back.

Alice laughed, and I joined in, and my heart journeyed down to my stomach and back again.

My grandmother did have grilled cheese sandwiches waiting for me, and when she saw Alice, she acted surprised for a moment and then became the hostess she prides herself on being.

"Would you like some milk? Some juice?" she asked, poking around the refrigerator.

"Water's fine, thank you," Alice answered, and after my grandmother got her a glass of ice water she disappeared, leaving Alice and me sitting in what grandmother calls the breakfast nook.

"This is good," Alice said, taking a bite.

"Yeah, it is," I said. "My grandmother's a really good cook."

"You've lived with her almost all your life?" Alice asked. "Ever since your parents died?"

"Yes," I answered, and I admired the way she just asked me directly about my mother and father. Not like grandmother's church friends who refer to my parents' "passing on" in some vague, strange way as if they just disappeared one day while out and about.

"Why were you guys living in Chicago, anyway?"

"My mother was a professor of history at Northwestern. My father worked in the education department at the Art Institute."

"Wow," Alice said. "Smart. But that makes sense, I guess. Where'd they meet?"

"In college. At Rice. Did you know my father was the first

143

and only student from Healy High ever to go there?" I said it not to brag, but just because it's always amazed me that one of the best schools in the country is a little over an hour away and no students from Healy attend or even apply.

"Maybe you'll go," Alice told me. "I'm sure someone as smart as you could get in, too."

I shrugged. I haven't thought much about where I'll go to school after my senior year. I'm sure my grandmother would love it if I went to Rice and stayed close by. Still, there's a part of me that would love to go to school in Chicago. When I told this to Alice, she asked if it was because I miss it.

"I don't remember it well enough to miss it," I said. "But I guess I feel on some level like I should go back there. Like it was my destiny to live there, and I need to let my destiny play out." I cringed inside for using the word *destiny*. I was afraid it made me look strange or like I was the type of nerd who plays Dungeons and Dragons.

But Alice just nodded like she understood. "You would have had such a different life if you'd stayed there, wouldn't you? I mean, you know. Educated parents. A big city. Lots of opportunities."

"That's true," I said. I'd only considered how different things would have been for me millions of times, even as I tried to make peace with my existence in Healy and the circumstances that brought me here. "Then again, I'm sure there would have been aspects of living in Chicago that I wouldn't have enjoyed. And I would have missed out on certain aspects of living here."

Alice snorted. "Like what?"

Like you. Of course I didn't dare say it.

"The way it's quiet in the evenings," I told her. "The way you can buy something at Seller Brothers and if you've forgotten your wallet they let you take what you need because they know you'll return and pay later. I don't know."

"You mean the way everyone knows your business," Alice said, and I realized this was the closest we'd ever come to really talking about what happened to her.

"Well, there's that. That's not pleasant. I know you know."

"No," Alice answered, her eyes not looking at me, her fingers carefully ripping the leftover crust of her sandwich into a small pile of crumbs. "It's not pleasant at all." Alice was quiet for a moment and then continued. "Sometimes I wonder what my life would have been like if my dad hadn't left. I mean, the way you must try and picture your life if your parents hadn't died."

"When did your father leave?" I asked. I didn't know anything about Alice's father.

"I guess he didn't really leave if he was never really here, right?" she said, shrugging her shoulders like that was meant as a familiar, funny punch line. "He was this guy my mom was dating over in Dove Lake. He worked as an auto mechanic. It was after she graduated from high school and she was working at becoming a dental hygienist. He was a friend of a friend or something from what my mom says. After she got pregnant, they moved in together and tried to make it work. But my mom says I cried so much as a baby. I had colic like crazy bad or something, and I would just scream and scream for hours. And I guess my father, his name was Hank, he couldn't take it anymore and told my mom he was sorry, but he wasn't ready to be a father."

"He sounds like a jerk," I said.

"I guess," Alice answered. The plate in front of her was nothing but crumbs, and I watched as she carefully flattened them with her right index finger. "But I still always wonder what life would have been like if things had gone differently. Like, what if I hadn't had colic? What if I had been the easiest baby in the world? I think my mom must think that sometimes."

"If he couldn't have handled colic, he couldn't have handled other things that would have come up," I told her, but I stopped because I could see in her expression that Alice didn't like to hear me criticize her father. She liked to imagine that things might have been better had he stayed. That her life would have been happier somehow.

"I'm such a cliché, aren't I?" Alice said, and she gave me a wry smirk. "Single mother. Absent father. Too many boyfriends, searching for love in all the wrong places and blah blah blah."

Sitting there with Alice and talking with her made me so content. So *satisfied*. So I gathered the guts and said, "Alice, you could never be a cliché. Not in a trillion years."

Alice looked at me with her gorgeous brown eyes and smiled. "A trillion years? Is that a scientifically proven number?"

I shrugged and smiled. "Yes," I said. "And I'm serious."

"Maybe you're right," she said. "But I have my doubts."

I wondered if this lunch, this conversation, would be the right time to bring up what Brandon had told me, but just as I was trying to figure out how to begin my story, she stretched her arms above her head and said, "Okay, this is getting too heavy-duty for me. I should probably go."

I worried for a moment that I'd scared her off, but as I walked her to the front door, she asked me if we could start up our tutoring sessions once school picked up. I was saddened by the fact that I wouldn't see Alice for two weeks, but I told her we could start tutoring again as soon as classes started back, and she thanked me once again for all the help.

As she headed out, I asked her if she needed a ride, but she said she wanted to walk.

"After all, what could happen to me in beautiful Healy, where everyone knows your name and your business?" She said this with sarcasm cutting through her voice, and I smiled at her.

"Now Alice," I joked, "don't you know nothing ever happens in Healy?"

"Not unless you're me," she said with a sigh, rolling her eyes, and after she turned, I watched her back as she made her way down the driveway. Then it hit me when she got to the street that she was going to have to walk in front of Brandon Fitzsimmons' house to get home. When we'd shown up at my house after school, we'd come in through the side door into the kitchen.

But right then she had to walk right past it. Right past his house and right past the red and white yard sign that read "BRANDON FITZSIMMONS * HEALY TIGER * WE WILL NEVER FORGET YOU!"

I watched as she headed down the sidewalk, and as she crossed in front of Brandon's house, I thought maybe it was the late December cold that made her reach back and pull her hood up over her head so far up you couldn't see her face anymore. But probably there was another reason.

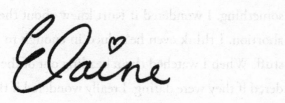

THE SLUT STALL HAS TAKEN ON A LIFE OF ITS own. I don't think Kelsie or any of us ever meant for it to get out of hand the way it did. I mean, it was so completely gross by Christmas I couldn't believe the stuff some people were writing. I only wrote in it that one time, the day Kelsie told us about Alice's abortion. But once was all it took. I told you people are always copying the things that I do.

I can't believe the school never cleaned it off. I can't believe Alice's mother never complained. It's weird how things can just get out of control sometimes. And it's weird how, like, when it's your job to be a popular bitch you just feel compelled to keep doing it sometimes. That sounds so lame and like a total excuse, I get it. But it is what it is.

Not too long ago, just before Winter Break, I saw Alice walking out of school with that super weirdo Kurt Morelli. They've been hanging out. Before everything happened, Alice walking around with Kurt Morelli would have been the equivalent of the Queen of England walking around with a homeless person or something. I wondered if Kurt knew about the Slut Stall or the abortion. I think even he's clued in enough to know about that stuff. When I watched them heading out of the building, I wondered if they were dating. I really wondered if they were sleeping together. Which would be kind of gross, but . . . anyway, it was odd to see them like that, together.

But in this strange way, it kind of made me feel less bad about everything. Don't get me wrong. There's this part of me that still really can't stand Alice and thinks she got everything that was coming to her. For fooling around with Brandon back in eighth grade. For standing there while Brandon read my diary. For sleeping with two guys at *my* party. For being responsible for Brandon's death.

But I guess there's this other part of me that wonders if maybe things have gone too far. I don't know. I keep thinking about that question my friend Maggie asked Kelsie that day we found out about Alice's abortion.

You don't even feel a little sorry for her?

It's sort of hard not to. Feel sorry for her, I mean. At least a little.

Something else that's happened recently other than Alice hanging out with Kurt is I stopped writing in my diary. I eventually dug it out of the closet and tried to write in it again, but it just felt stupid somehow. A diary is supposed to be private, and even though the only person who'd read it other than me was dead, it still felt weird, so I ripped out every page and sent it through the shredder my dad keeps in his study. And then I put all the shredded pieces in a bag and dumped it in our neighbor's trash can. Just in case.

Despite how odd this year has been in many ways, the thing is, I like it here and I don't ever want to leave. I want to go to UT and then marry a guy who wants to stay in Healy forever and I want him to take over the business from my dad and I'll help run it, and I want to have a daughter who's just like me, and I'll join Healy Boosters and be the dance squad mom and help out during the Christmas Carnival and all of that.

I know what you're thinking. So lame. So small town. But *why* is it lame? Why is it lame to want to be in a place that feels safe to you and that you like? I'm not an idiot. I have a B+ average and I watch the local news every morning while I'm eating my oatmeal and blueberries (Weight Watchers points = 4). I can name both of my senators and I understand how payroll taxes work on account of I've worked at my dad's shop every summer since I was thirteen and I can probably find most major countries on a map if you give me a second.

I remember sophomore year when the Fashion Club went on a school trip to New York City. And our tour guide at the museum at the Fashion Institute of Technology smiled in this super pitying way when we told her where we were from. I mean, it's one thing to be from Texas, but they really think you're a hay-seed if you're not from Houston or Dallas or something. Or at least San Antonio.

"Healy? I think you're my first group from there. And how many people live in Healy?" She was talking super slowly to us. I thought New Yorkers were supposed to talk fast.

"A little over 3,000," my teacher said.

"Oh my! I think that's how many people are in my building!" Ha-ha.

Alice Franklin had been on that trip. She'd saved her babysitting money and her Healy Pool North money to pay for it. I remember how when the tour guide said that, I looked over at her and we both rolled our eyes at each other.

If I'd grown up in Manhattan and I wanted to stay in Manhattan and never leave because I felt safe there and I liked it, nobody would think twice. People would think I was sophisticated, probably. And why? Because they have a subway system? Because there's more than one movie theater? Because of the lions in front of the New York Public Library? (Yeah, I know about those, too.) I honestly don't get the difference. If I'd been born in Manhattan, I probably would have wanted to stay there just like I want to stay in Healy. And honestly, even in Manhattan I think I still would have been considered popular. And I'm not so small town that I don't realize that even in Manhattan, a girl like Alice Franklin would still have been considered a slut.

I forgot. There's one other big thing that's happened this year. I finally stopped going to Weight Watchers.

Right after the holidays my mom came into my room early one Saturday wearing her weigh-in clothes. She always wears these cotton pajama pants and a tank top to every meeting because she's convinced that they only weigh, like, half an ounce. She'd been all stressed out because over Christmas she'd eaten three thousand candy canes and twenty gallons of eggnog or whatever.

"Elaine, meeting," she said. "Time to get up."

Like most of the things I do, I can't really tell you why I did it, but I pulled the covers up over my head and said, "I'm not going."

"What?"

I was staring at the tiny pink flowers on my sheets. I focused in on one and stared it down.

"I'm not going," I said again.

"Elaine, why? You've had such a great week. I saw your food tracker and you've eaten beneath your daily points target every day!"

And I'm starving, I thought to myself. *And if I eat any more Greek yogurt I'm going to become Greek.*

"I just don't want to go," I said.

"Would you at least take those covers off your head?"

I thought I would totally lose my nerve or something if I had to look her in the eyes, but I did take the covers off my head and I did stare at her and I did say again, "I just don't want to go."

My mom did this deep breath thing and tried to smile, but I could tell she was ticked off. The deal with my mom is that she's always trying to be my friend, so I could tell she was debating in her head whether or not she should make me go or just pretend that this week was only this weird break in our gal pal routine.

"I just know you've had a loss, if that's what you're worried about," she said.

I dug my hands under my covers and I squeezed the pink-flowered sheets and said, "Mom, I'm not going. I'm not going today, and the thing is, I'm not going next week either. I'm not going to Weight Watchers anymore because I don't want to and I don't need to. If you want to go, that's cool, okay? But I'm not going."

Okay. There. I said it.

My mom did this whole pouty face thing, and I knew she would ignore me for the rest of the day. She turned around and left me alone, and after she walked away, I fell back against my pillows, pretty much totally in awe of myself.

No more holding my breath during weigh-ins. No more listening to old ladies talk about spraying their pizzas with Lysol so they wouldn't eat them. No more low-point substitutes that taste like crap when you compare them to the real thing. No more no more no more.

I waited until I heard my mom back her SUV out of the driveway. I knew my dad was still asleep. I went downstairs and found a box of S'Mores Pop-Tarts in my dad's section of the food pantry and I took it back up to my room, crawled into bed, and ate all six of them in ten minutes. The chocolate icing melted on my tongue and the marshmallow filling seemed to be made of nothing but sugar and lard. I didn't even need to toast them. I just ate them, and I loved every single bite.

When I was done eating, I patted my stomach. Then I looked out the window by my bed down onto my street that goes past the Nealy house and the Carver house until it curves down and around a corner. I couldn't see past that corner, but I know all of the houses beyond it and I know all of the people who live in them. Just like I know what and who is around every corner of every street in Healy. And this fact, like the box of S'Mores, made me very happy. It made me, like, completely content.

I tossed the empty box into the garbage can where I knew my mom would find it eventually, and I slid back under the covers and fell asleep.

Kelsie

THE DAY BEFORE WINTER BREAK IS ALWAYS A half day. It's also the world's most pointless school day. Maybe even more pointless than the last day of school. At least on the last day there can be no reason for assigning homework or taking attendance. But the half day before Winter Break is always this total exercise in killing time.

Right before the end of the day, I was stuck in Chemistry and totally bored out of my mind. So I asked to go to the bathroom. I ended up in the bathroom with the Slut Stall. It's not like we don't use it all the time or anything.

But normally when I go in there, Alice Franklin isn't actually inside the bathroom, washing her hands.

I walked in and I saw her and almost immediately I wanted to turn around and walk out, but I knew that would be totally and completely chicken of me. I'd done what I'd done, and I couldn't take it back.

I didn't actually have to go to the bathroom. My plan had been to go in and text someone or fool around on my phone or just basically kill time in any other place besides Chemistry class.

But there was Alice Franklin, my former best friend, dressed in that bulky weird sweatshirt and reaching for some paper towels. When I walked in, she lifted her head up and looked right at me. Right into my eyes.

There was nothing to say. I just stood there for a second and then I went into a stall. Not the Slut Stall. A different one. I tried to pee, and I couldn't. I waited for at least five minutes. I thought I could outwait Alice, but when I heard her tell some girl who walked in after me to get out and that she wanted the bathroom to herself, I knew there wasn't anything I could do except face her. I came back out and Alice was standing there, staring at me. Her dark brown eyes were just penetrating into me. My heart was racing. I felt sick.

"Why did you tell everyone I had an abortion?" Alice said evenly. Now my heart was thumping so loudly I was sure Alice could hear it. It was like that weird short story we read in English class about the guy who was convinced he could hear the heart of his murder victim underneath the floorboards.

I didn't answer. I just stood there. Heart thumping.

"Why are you telling everyone that I had an abortion when you *know* it's not true?" Alice said. Her cheeks were all red and blotchy, and she was breathing hard. She could be mad at me about so many things. Ditching her. Ignoring her. Starting the Slut Stall. But right then it was the abortion rumor she was the maddest about. And I couldn't blame her.

"I . . ." I said. I couldn't talk. Like I said, there was nothing to say. Nothing.

"Look," Alice said, and for a second I wondered if she was going to hit me. It's not like I didn't deserve it. But she just stayed there by the sink, and I stood back, up against the stall door, as far from her as I could be. She kept talking, her voice low, steady, but I could tell it sounded like it was about to explode. "I get the fact that I can't do anything about the crap going around about me and Brandon and Tommy. I get that. Okay. And I get the fact that no one would even think for a second that the amazing and wonderful Josh Waverly made up that story about me texting Brandon in the truck and causing the accident. Fine. People are going to think what they're going to think and it doesn't matter what I say about it. But you *know* the abortion thing is a lie. You *know* it!" When Alice said *know* the second time, she kind of hit the edge of the white porcelain sink with her hand, and I jumped a little.

"I . . ." I said, and Alice stood there, like she was just begging me with her eyes to say something, anything. And I couldn't. I really couldn't.

All of a sudden Alice was crying. Not all sobbing or anything, but there were tears running down her face. Her voice stayed really even though, just even and steady despite all the tears.

"You were my best friend, Kelsie. My *best friend*. And I am not letting you out of here until you tell me why you made that up," she whispered, stepping toward me. "You can't just lie like that!"

I swallowed. Now I was the one breathing hard. I was pretty sure I was red in the face, too.

"Well, you lied to me once," I said, barely getting the words out. "You lied to me about messing around with Mark Lopez that summer at the pool. You said I wouldn't understand because I was a *virgin*." I spat out the word *virgin* like I had as much right to be mad at Alice as she had to be mad at me.

Alice stared at me, completely confused, like she'd made up all sorts of reasons why I did what I did, but in a million years that had never been one of them. She sort of shook her head a little, like she was repeating my words in her head.

"Mark Lopez? That was a million years ago. I don't . . . what does that have to do with . . ." She just stood there. Stunned, I guess. I just kept swallowing and breathing hard and my heart was thumping so bad I just knew Alice could hear it.

And for the briefest moment, the teeniest, tiniest moment ever, I was totally tempted to tell Alice everything. Like, everything. Like real best friends are supposed to do. About how I'd felt like I'd had something to prove after she said what she'd said. How I got jealous of her so much of the time. How I'd had sex with Tommy Cray. How I'd been terrified I'd lose all my friends by hanging out with her and I'd be transformed into a dork again. I even wanted to tell her about the abortion. Because she was hurting so bad and I was hurting so bad—*am* hurting so bad—and, like, I just wished I had someone I could talk to. Anyone. But I knew I wouldn't say anything to her. I'm not that brave. I'm just not.

And not only am I not a brave person, to tell you the truth sometimes I'm pretty sure I'm the worst person alive.

We didn't say anything for a minute, and Alice stopped crying. She looked confused. Then she walked past me into the stall and got some toilet paper and patted the skin under her eyes. When she came back out, she just stared at me and said really slowly, like I was stupid: "Okay. So you told the entire school I had an abortion because one time—over a year ago—I lied to you about giving Mark Lopez a blow job because I felt stupid about it? *That's* why you told everyone I had an *abortion*?"

"And you said I was a virgin," I repeated. Oh God, that sounded so dumb. So impossibly dumb.

"Well . . . you are," Alice said, still dragging out her words like I was a kindergartner. "Right?"

Here was my chance to make it better. Here was my chance to tell the truth. To fix everything.

But I couldn't. Yeah, I was scared of becoming Kelsie from Flint again. But maybe just as much—as silly as I know it sounds, as ridiculous as I know it is—there was a part of me that blamed Alice Franklin for The Really Awful Stuff. It was petty and childish and I realize that. My mom was more to blame than Alice, and I was probably the most to blame out of everyone. But at that moment in the bathroom I couldn't help but think that maybe things would have turned out different if Alice hadn't made me feel like a naive little kid about everything.

Maybe.

So I didn't tell her the truth. I didn't fix anything. I just stood there.

"Okay," Alice said. Then she added, "So tell me to my face that you know the abortion thing is a lie."

I nodded yes. "It's a lie," I whispered. "I made it up."

Alice didn't look *satisfied* or anything. She just stood there, almost like she couldn't believe she'd gotten me to say what I said. Then she walked over to the corner of the bathroom and threw away the wadded-up toilet paper she'd used to dry her face. Then she turned around to face me again.

"You know what, Kelsie?" Alice said all calm. "Fuck you." She stood there and looked at me evenly for another moment. When she said that last part, her voice broke like she might cry again, but she didn't. And then she just walked out.

I stood there for a second after the swinging door shushed shut, and I walked into the Slut Stall.

Killer Alice did it with Santa Claus. Merry Christmas HO HO HO!

I sat on the toilet and I pulled my legs up under me. I put my chin on my knees. I cried so hard, and it felt so good. It felt *so* good. I cried until snot was just pouring down my nose and into my mouth. I sobbed and I sobbed and I sobbed. Someone whose voice I didn't recognize came in and asked me through the door if I was okay, and I didn't answer. I didn't even try to stop sobbing. I just kept crying.

Finally, when I realized whoever came in might go get a teacher or something, I pulled it together and came out and washed my face. I walked down the hallway and out of one of the side doors of the building and started walking toward my house. It's so easy to cut school at Healy High. I don't think my Chemistry teacher even noticed I never came back. I just walked toward home. I didn't even have my backpack or my coat—I left them both in my locker—but I didn't care. The only thing that mattered was leaving that building as fast as I could.

I feel like the baby was a boy. I don't know why. I just do. I have no reason to think that or anything. Maybe I feel that way just because I wanted it to be.

If I ever get pregnant again, I hope it's a boy. I would say I'll pray it's a boy, but I don't know if God listens to me anymore. It's scary to say this, but I don't know if God exists, to tell you the truth.

But if I do end up having a girl, there are so many things I'll do for her. So many things I swear I'll do for her.

I'll never walk into her room without knocking.

I won't fake emotions in front of her.

I'll tell her she's special just because she's who she is.

I won't act like I'm perfect.

I won't scare her. I won't let her be scared of me.

I won't tell her I know all the answers.

I won't lie to her.

And if she ever feels awful or scared or alone or goes through something terrible and miserable and horrible, I won't leave her in her room all by herself. No, I'll crawl into bed with her and hold her in my arms, and I'll let her cry and cry all she wants, and I'll press her little head into my neck and let her sob tears on me, and I won't tell her I know it will get better, and I won't promise her she won't always feel this bad, and I won't make her stop crying. I'll let her cry for as long as she needs to. As long as she needs to. As long as she needs to.

WHEN I ARRIVED AT ALICE'S HOUSE THAT early spring evening, Alice greeted me with a smile at the door and said, "So, I have a surprise!" Oh, to have a quick wit about me, to be able to respond with some clever answer. But I just followed her into the kitchen and asked, "What?"

"Look!" Alice said, pulling out a math quiz from her binder. Her face was gleeful. "An 88! Do you know how crazy this is for me? An 88!" Next to the circled grade Mr. Commons had written "Much Improved!" and underlined it.

I was thrilled and also upset. Upset that this 88 meant Alice would most likely no longer be requesting my help in mathematics. Gone would be our once or even twice weekly visits together. Gone would be the nights I could soak in her face, her eyes, her smile, the way she grips her pencil and bites her bottom lip as she works, the way she grins to herself when she gets something right.

Gone would be our conversations. The ones that—ever since the day we had lunch together at my house—have more frequently started meandering away from talk of constants and variables and begun entering into other territories. Our families. Our likes and dislikes. Our favorite things. Our funny habits.

I know, for instance, that Alice still holds her breath when she walks past the historic city cemetery on the way home from school, even though she knows it's a silly superstition. And Alice knows, for example, that elevators make me claustrophobic. ("So I suppose it's a good thing that we only have two of them in Healy," Alice observed with a laugh.) And I know, for instance, that Alice's mother is dating a man over in Clayton and sometimes leaves Alice all alone for a week at a time. ("Once she forgot to pay the power bill and I had to get ready for school in the dark, if you can believe it," she confessed with a shrug, like she was used to such annoyances when dealing with her mother.) And Alice knows that back in first grade I liked to imagine that young, pretty Miss Sweeney could somehow become my mother since my real mother was gone. When I told that to Alice, she smiled at me.

"You know what? I kind of used to imagine that, too," Alice admitted.

But now, all of that sharing will be going away. Because of a wonderful, terrible 88.

I supposed my expression must have given away my sadness because Alice's face—her beautiful face—turned from excited to confused.

"Oh," she said, her voice soft. "Do you . . . you think I . . . I mean, I should be getting As?" Then she smiled. "Kurt, it's nice to have your faith in me, but come on. An 88! You've got to be happy over this. We worked so hard."

"No, Alice, I am," I said. "I'm very happy for you. But I'm just . . ." I took a breath. I could tell Alice how I felt. I could do it. "I guess I'm just worried that maybe you won't need my help anymore."

Alice sat down at the kitchen table, so I did, too. She stared at the 88 and then back at me. "But I'm not, I mean . . . I'm not paying you to do this. Why would you . . ." She stopped, and her cheeks pinked up a bit. Alice knows I'm attracted to her. She knows and she knows I know she knows. Even earlier in the fall when she'd asked me if I was only tutoring her because I wanted to sleep with her, she must have known deep down inside that I liked her.

Hadn't she realized that as time went by, it wasn't simply sex that I thought about? (Although I would be a hypocrite and a liar if I didn't admit to frequently fantasizing about such un-attainable acts in the privacy of my own home.) Hadn't she figured out by now that I really like her—*her*, Alice? Not Fantasy Alice, but the living, breathing, talking, walking, actual Alice who holds her breath near cemeteries and eats grilled cheese sandwiches and has managed to survive complete and utter banishment from everyone she ever regarded as a friend and still come to school every single day.

That Alice. I like her. I like being her friend.

Alice didn't humiliate me. She didn't make me elaborate. She just sat there, pink cheeks, 88 in hand.

"Alice, I know that I'm not . . . I mean, that I'm not exactly what you'd find . . ." I could not find the words. I have a genius IQ, yet I could not find the words.

Alice could. She reached out across the kitchen table and put her small girl hand on top of my arm, and the warmth that pulsed from that touch heated up my entire body from my toes to the roots of my hair.

"Kurt, it's okay. I want you to know that I don't know what I would have done this year without you. And I don't mean just math. I mean, that was great. But what I mean is that you were the only person in the school who would even talk to me. You were my friend, Kurt. You *are* my friend. And I don't have any friends other than you. None. I don't know if you know what that feels like," she said, and as she said it, her voice broke a bit.

"Yes," I said. "I do. I know exactly what that feels like."

Alice looked ashamed as if she should have predicted such an answer. She glanced down and blushed harder.

"Of course you know," she said. "I suck, I'm sorry. God, until everything happened, I never even gave you the time of day."

"That's not true," I said. "When I helped you with your Geometry that one time in the library back in tenth grade, you were very nice to me."

Alice let go of my hand and wiped away the tears that were beginning to fall.

"Oh sure, I was nice, but I just . . ." She hesitated. "I saw you as this weird nerd. This weird nerd who could be useful to me in the moment. I probably wouldn't have been nice to you otherwise. I'm sorry, but that's the truth. You can hate me for admitting it."

It hurt to hear despite knowing it was the truth, but I didn't hate Alice. I couldn't and I can't.

"I don't think someone like Elaine O'Dea would have been nice to me," I argued. "Even if she only saw me as a useful nerd. You must have known that I would have helped you with your Geometry regardless. The fact that you were nice to me even when you didn't have to be . . . I mean, that has to count for something, right?"

Alice slowed down her crying and smiled at me.

"Kurt, you're too nice. I'm not a saint, you know. I've done some stupid, messed-up stuff in my life."

"I know," I told her. "But it's not like my motives were entirely pure."

"What do you mean?"

I stared at my shoes, swallowed hard, and said, "Well, I did want to help you with your math, that's true. But I don't think I would have done it if I hadn't thought you were so beautiful."

Alice didn't say anything for what seemed like an unfairly long amount of time. Then she asked me, "So . . . if I got attacked by a mountain lion and my face was all gross and disfigured, and, like, ripped to shreds, you wouldn't have helped me with my math homework?" I think maybe she was trying not to laugh.

"Truth?" I said, digging around for the courage to look at her. "In the beginning, no. I wouldn't have. But now you could go out and get mauled by twenty mountain lions, and I would still want to help you. I would still want to be your friend. You're a great person, Alice. You're not just beautiful."

Alice smiled her wide smile. The crooked incisor smile.

"Well I guess we've both, like, evolved or whatever." She laughed and then stood up with a long exhale and a stretch of her arms. "I'm sorry, but this conversation calls for shitty beer."

I nodded in agreement and took the cold can of Lone Star that Alice handed me from the refrigerator. She popped her can open and took a sip.

"I'm so glad you want to be my friend," she laughed. "Even though I've had seven abortions and slept with the principal and plotted to have Brandon Fitzsimmons murdered by Mafia hit men before killing him with my dirty texting, right?" Alice rolled her eyes. It was the first time she'd ever said his name out loud in front of me, and suddenly, I knew it was time. It had to be now or never.

"Alice, about Brandon Fitzsimmons," I said, and I took another sip of beer in an effort not to lose courage. "There's something I've been meaning to tell you. Something I think you'd like to know."

JOSH

WE HAD OUR WORST SEASON IN A REALLY
long time. It just sucked. We won that first game against Dominion. Maybe they let us win because they felt sorry for us
because of Brandon. I don't know. But we lost almost every game
after that except for the one against Pikesville, and I don't even
think that counts because that town is so small they barely have
enough guys to make up a team.

Coach Hendricks was always bringing up Brandon in the
locker room. At least in the beginning of the season when we
still had a chance. He'd say things like, "Brandon would have
wanted us to go and give it our all!" or "Let's win this one for
Brandon!" Whatever. It pissed me off. Because really, Coach
Hendricks just wanted us to win. He was upset Brandon was
dead because Brandon was the best quarterback Healy had had
in a million years. But he wasn't upset Brandon was dead because

of anything else about Brandon. And so it really bugged me the way he kept bringing him up all the time. I figured if Brandon could see what was going on from heaven, it would piss him off, too.

I sort of want to believe in heaven. I think about it whenever Reverend Simmons talks about it at church on Sunday. I want to believe I'll see Brandon again, and in heaven we can pass footballs all day and drink good beer for free and just chill. I guess for a little while I had heaven on earth, because that's what Brandon and I did most of the time, just hung out. Drinking, chilling. Whatever. We didn't even pay for the beer because we stole it from our parents.

But if you want to know the truth, I have this feeling down in my gut that there is no heaven. My gut just tells me it doesn't make sense. How could there be a heaven for me and not for every little fly I swat or squirrel I've accidentally run over? But it makes me feel really weird thinking about death just being it, the end. So whenever the idea of no heaven comes into my head, I just sort of try and push it out of there.

I try not to think about that stuff too much.

And the truth is, even if there is a heaven, I don't think I'll get in. Because even more than trying not to think about Brandon and heaven, what I really try not to think about is what actually happened the day of the accident. The day after the Homecoming Game. I've never told anyone about it, and it's a weird feeling to know I never will. Never.

We were drinking beers on Brandon's roof. Some hair of the

dog, I guess, and I was drinking double everything that Brandon was putting down. Brandon had three, maybe four beers if you want to know the truth, so he was pretty buzzed when his mom asked us to run to the store for her to get her some diapers for Brandon's little sister. That's why the cops said his blood alcohol was probably the cause of the accident. But I'd seen Brandon drive after drinking way more than that. He drove drunk all the time. It's just a Healy thing, I guess. It was hot out, and the inside of Brandon's truck was like a million degrees. Brandon stripped his shirt off when we got inside and cranked open the windows.

"AC's broke again," he said.

My head was loopy from the beer. I knew my eyes were looking at Brandon's chest for too long. I'd seen Brandon's chest more times than I could count. In the locker room. When he stayed over at my house. Swimming at Healy Pool North. I looked one last time as we were getting in the truck and then I told myself to stop looking.

I was pretty lit and feeling good, and it sounds stupid when I say it now, but as we pulled out of Brandon's front yard I just thought about us winning the Homecoming Game and everybody loving us and thinking how great we were. It was like I was high on us being us. Me and Brandon. Brandon and me.

"We're kings of this town, man," I said as Brandon picked up speed. The trees were blobs of green. The oncoming traffic was flashes of color. Red truck. Blue car. White van. The air coming in the windows was coming in so fast it was like it was cutting into our faces. But it felt good.

"Hell, yeah, we're kings of this town," Brandon said, and it was so cool to be just the two of us, alone together. I mean, I was Brandon's best friend, but people were always trying to get near him. I guess what I mean is that sometimes it was nice when it was just the two of us all by ourselves. Like that moment in the truck. It felt perfect.

But then Brandon took out his phone.

"I think this king needs a queen," he said. His eyes kept darting between the phone and the road.

"What, dude?" I said, raising my voice so he could hear me over the wind coming in through the windows.

"I need to get laid," Brandon yelled, laughing. "Now where the hell is Alice Franklin's number?"

I stared out the window. Green blobs of trees. Pink blobs of houses. The rev of the engine building and building. I didn't want Brandon to text Alice Franklin. I didn't want him to text any girl. I wanted it to be just us. I know it sounds so stupid, but I felt jealous. Like Alice was right there in the cab of the truck with us. Like all the girls who loved Brandon, which was basically every girl in Healy, were in the cab of the truck with us. And for that one moment I just didn't want them around.

"Poor Alice might be ripe for a little attention, don't you think?" Brandon said, his eyes jumping between County Road 181 and his cell. "She's seemed kinda lonely lately. People keep giving her shit." He grinned at me, and we both knew he was thinking about Elaine's party. My mind went back to that night. To Alice sitting on Brandon's lap and going upstairs with him and having sex with him. And do you know what I did?

I reached over and grabbed Brandon's phone right out of his hands.

"What the hell?" Brandon said, turning to look at me. And if I'm honest, the very last thing I remember before the crash is the expression on Brandon's face when I took his phone away. I knew he was pissed off at me, which he never was. I never made him mad. But right then, I did.

I was sitting there, holding his phone in my hands, and it was like Brandon suddenly remembered he was supposed to be driving. He turned back to the road, and then the next thing I heard was the screech of the brakes.

When Mrs. Fitzsimmons came over to see me after Brandon's funeral, I never thought what I said about Alice would explode like it did. But when Brandon's mom pushed me and pushed me to tell her every detail about the accident, the idea of blaming Alice popped into my head. It felt like the easiest way to get her off my back. And the truth is, it sort of helped ease the guilt a little at that moment. I mean, Brandon was drunk, and maybe that really is why he crashed the truck. When I'm having an okay day I think to myself, yeah, that's probably it. It had nothing to do with me. But when I'm having a not-so-okay day, which, honestly, is a lot of the time . . . well then I think Brandon's dying *was* all my fault. If I hadn't grabbed that phone, maybe he would still be alive. Maybe we'd be sitting around drinking beers on his roof and talking about being state champs our senior year. I don't know for sure, and what sucks so bad is I'll never know.

But something I do know for sure is that Alice Franklin never texted Brandon Fitzsimmons. Not even once.

Back in the fall Alice started hanging around with the skinny, smart dude who lives next door to Brandon's family, Kurt Morelli. Brandon always liked messing with him, but Kurt always took it real good and everything, like he didn't mind. He was always just kind of his own guy, and I always sort of admired the fact that he didn't really care if he had friends or not. Like he was all he needed. The funny thing is we all hung out together back in elementary school before we figured out who was popular and who wasn't. I remember Kurt coming over to Brandon's house when we were in second or third grade and we all threw water balloons off the roof in front of Brandon's bedroom window and Brandon's mom found out and had a heart attack over it. And Kurt, that dude was so smart, he actually tried to explain to Mrs. Fitzsimmons that the roof was safe by explaining some crap about its structure. Some physics crap, I don't know.

Anyway, it's weird to think about that. About the three of us being together. We called it playing back then. Like, do you want to come over and play? Sounds so corny. And then it all stopped. And now Brandon is dead and Kurt is hanging out with Alice Franklin and I don't talk to either of them. It's weird. But maybe they'll be friends. I don't know. I guess I kind of hope so.

Speaking of friends, I guess Brandon really was my best one because since the accident, I basically feel empty inside. I mean, the guys on the team are okay and everything, and I still go to parties and girls still try to get all over me and everything, and I still get drunk and hang out in the Healy High parking lot most weekends. But it's just not the same. Nothing is the same without Brandon. I still use his locker. It's closer to all of my classes, and I knew the combination and the school didn't assign anyone else to it or anything after he died, so I use it pretty much every day. His mom and dad cleaned it out after the accident, but I remembered to get there beforehand and rip out all the pictures of girls in bikinis and some other crap they maybe wouldn't want to see. So it's not like there's anything of him in there anymore. But I guess I still just like using it. I don't know. Sometimes I think I can hear him walking up behind me, giving me shit for using his locker. Once I even turned around because I was so sure I was going to see him. Maybe I'm losing it.

But mostly I just go through every day and I do what people expect of me. I go to class. I get Cs. I eat in the cafeteria. I laugh at the stupid gross jokes the other guys make. I go home. I talk to my parents about basic stuff. I go to church. I ask God to forgive me and take care of things and keep everybody safe.

But life just isn't the same without Brandon. It's not as much fun. I mean, look, I'm not crazy smart, but I'm not so dumb that I don't realize that Brandon could be kind of a dick sometimes. He could be. He pretty much could afford to be a dick and nobody questioned him or anything. So he could make fun of kids like Kurt Morelli and teachers didn't call him on it. He could screw Alice Franklin and then get Tommy Cray to screw her, too, on the very same night, and nobody would say anything bad about him. They'd only talk bad about Alice. Don't think that I thought that crap was cool. I know it wasn't.

But Brandon Fitzsimmons could be really funny. He could be really great. He really was my friend. He was always really nice to my brother whenever he hung out at my house, like playing video games with him and letting my brother beat him just because. He never made me feel bad about anything. Not even about not sleeping with lots of girls, and not about not being that quick to get things. He didn't even give me a hard time sophomore year when I missed his pass and I lost us the game against Clayton.

It was our first year on varsity and the older guys had been pissed that two tenth graders were quarterback and wide receiver—even if we had been good enough to deserve it and they knew it. I still think about that game. We were down by three and there were ten seconds on the clock. Brandon had to throw long and he looked me right in the eyes in the huddle. It was our one chance. He knew I knew what he was thinking.

We'd practiced throws so many times. I could catch any of his throws with my eyes closed. Literally. Sometimes I would dream about catching his throws. Swish, thump. Swish, thump.

That night, right before the big play, there was no sound in my ears. Just like there never is during a big moment in a game. There was just me, and the smell of the grassy field, and the thud in my chest as I got ready to run.

It was a perfect spiral. It was a perfect Brandon throw. It was like every throw we practiced in my yard or his yard or after practice on the field. Like I said, it was perfect.

And I missed it.

I don't know how. Not even today could I tell you how or why I missed it. But I did. I crashed into the end zone and the ball landed next to me. I still grabbed it. Like somehow that would make everything okay. I still grabbed the ball like a moron.

Man, people gave me shit over that for weeks. I was benched for the next game. I mean, my own dad was all over me for it.

But not Brandon. Not even once.

"Dude, it happens to everybody," Brandon had said that night in the locker room after some of the seniors had given me grief and Coach Hendricks had acted like I didn't even exist.

"It doesn't happen to *me*," I answered. "Not when you throw like you throw. That was a perfect ball and I missed it. Damn it!" I punched my locker with my fist and it didn't even hurt I was so mad.

Brandon put his hand on my shoulder. My pads were off and I was naked from the waist up. My body ached like it always does after a game, but I can still remember now how good it felt to have Brandon's grip on my shoulder. Like a steady weight. Like a small hug.

"Look, man, it isn't anything. Don't let this mess with you, man," he whispered, right into my ear. "You and me, we're gonna take this team to state by senior year. I'm not kidding around, man. We're gonna do it and you know it. Now shake this off, buddy."

Of course, we never got the chance to. Take the team to state, I mean. But that's the moment I try to think about when I think about Brandon Fitzsimmons. Not those last, stupid, crazy moments in the truck or my lies about him and Alice. I try to think about his whisper in my ear. He could be a jerk sometimes, I admit it. But he could also be a real friend. He was my best friend, and I'm so sorry he's gone. I wish like hell that he was still around.

Kurt

AS I EXPLAINED TO ALICE ABOUT THE NIGHT on the rooftop with Brandon so many months ago, I could tell she wasn't reacting well. I could see how quickly the warm, friendly moment we'd just shared was leaving us. First of all, she kept bringing her eyebrows together in a frown. Second, she finished the can of Lone Star too quickly and stood up to get another one before I was halfway done with the story. Third, when I finally finished illustrating—in halting, nervous words—the fact that Brandon had admitted to me that the entire event at Elaine's party had been a lie and I had known this all along, all throughout our young friendship, Alice Franklin exhaled and then said softly, almost as if she were about to laugh at something that wasn't funny at all: "Are you kidding me?"

I said nothing. I simply swallowed and nodded. It was over. I knew that right then.

"Wow," Alice said, her expression darting between wounded and angry, "is there anyone in this crappy town that I can trust for more than five seconds?"

I wanted to tell her there had never been a time she couldn't trust me and there never would be. It made me ache that she couldn't see that. But confusion rested on Alice's face; it was the same expression I had seen when she worked out a difficult math problem. She rubbed her thumb up and down the side of the can of Lone Star. Finally, she spoke.

"So you're saying you had information that could have, like, cleared my name and you didn't . . ." Her voice trailed off. She broke eye contact with me and stared blankly at the kitchen table. "Not that it would have mattered, I guess." That last part came out sounding as if she'd forgotten I was even sitting there. Detached. Almost cold.

"Alice, I just could never figure out the right time to tell you," I said, surprised that I had the courage to keep trying to explain myself. And somewhat frustrated that I even needed to—that she couldn't see just a sliver of my side of the story. "I wanted to tell you, but at the same time, we barely knew each other when I started helping you with math. And then as we grew closer, I wasn't sure how to approach you about it. I almost did, that night I gave you your Christmas present. And the day we had grilled cheese sandwiches at my house. And about a dozen times in between."

"And you didn't because why?" Her voice was almost a whisper.

"Because the longer time went on without me saying anything, the stupider it seemed that I'd never said anything at all," I explained. "And I was afraid *this* might happen." At the word *this*, I motioned with my hand at the space between us. I could feel it widening by the moment.

"Well I guess it is happening," Alice said, and I crumpled inside as I saw her eyes grow glassy with tears.

My heart was collapsing.

"Alice, if you want, I'll put it out there. I'll put it online. I'll take out ads in the paper. I'll hang banners from the front of the school."

"And what are they going to say, 'Alice Franklin Is Not a Slut'?" She squeezed her eyes shut to keep back the tears and then opened them and looked right at me. Then, in a voice she might have used in her past, she said, "Besides, who would believe *you*?" A huff escaped from her lips and she crossed her arms in front of her. And then she laughed a little. A cutting, mocking laugh.

The laugh was what hurt the most.

I attempted to ignore the sting of it and the obvious implication that the *you* Alice was referring to—that, of course, would be *me*—was nothing more than parasitic scum. But it was impossible. I tried to tell myself that Alice's words were coming from a place of hurt, but I was angry with her. I wanted to shrug off how I felt, but I couldn't.

Because for the first time ever when it came to Alice, I felt something I hadn't felt before.

Used.

"How can you say that to me?" I heard myself asking, voice quaking. "How? How could you ever question that I don't feel terrible about this? That I wouldn't do anything for you? After all these months? After everything?"

Alice just sat there at the kitchen table with the chipped yellow Formica and the two cans of Lone Star beer in front of her. She wouldn't look at me. She wouldn't acknowledge me at all. All she did was roll her eyes.

I reached for my bag and my car keys.

"Alice," I said, taking a deep breath, "I know that you, of all people, recognize that life isn't fair. That life can be cruel, arbitrary even. So maybe it's wrong for me to ask you to recognize the unfairness of this situation. Because this isn't fair, the way you're treating me right now. This isn't right."

In a sharp voice she snapped, "Why don't you get out?"

"I was already leaving," I told her.

And I did.

Elaine

MISTY HAS BEEN DOING MY HAIR SINCE I was in fifth grade, and she's only ever screwed up once. And that was technically my fault since I told her to give me bangs and I look absurd with bangs. Anyway, Misty's been doing my hair since I cared about having my hair done, so when I needed it done for the last dance of the year, of course I booked her early. And of course I expected to have to sit around at the salon because Misty is always running at least thirty minutes behind.

What I didn't expect when I showed up on the Saturday of the dance was Alice Franklin sitting in the waiting area of the Curl Up and Dye, flipping through some ancient copy of *Teen Vogue*.

I don't know why. I mean, Alice still had hair after everything that happened. She still needed to get it cut, obviously.

But all I could think of when I walked in was, okay, this is random and awkward.

She looked up when she heard the jangle of the bells hanging off the door handle and then looked back down at the *Teen Vogue* super fast like she was oblivious to my presence. But her cheeks reddened a little, and she was doing that thing where you act like you're reading but you're so clearly not. I could hear Misty in the back room, chatting away with somebody. There wasn't anyone at the front desk. It was just me and Alice. I picked up a copy of *Cosmo* and started turning pages.

After about two minutes I just couldn't stand the silence anymore. Frankly, it was too weird. Maybe it was all the chemicals Misty uses. Maybe it was the fact that I'd already read that issue of *Cosmo* which I was holding in my hands. But all of a sudden, I was talking to Alice Franklin. For the very first time since my party almost a year ago.

"Do you have a one o'clock?" I asked.

Alice brought her gaze up over the top of the *Teen Vogue* and I know I saw her eyebrows jump up a bit like she was surprised I'd said anything. To be honest, I was surprised myself. Alice looked back down at the magazine and said, "Try twelve thirty."

"Oh my God, seriously?"

"Yes."

"God."

Total silence.

I put down my *Cosmo* and crossed my arms over my chest. Alice still wouldn't look at me.

"Who's back there taking so long anyway?" I asked.

Alice waited a second before responding. "Ms. Cooper."

"Oh God," I groaned. "We'll be here all day." Ms. Cooper was the Healy High secretary, and she was always trying to get us to believe she was a real redhead. She so wasn't.

Alice snapped her magazine shut and stared at me. "Why are you talking to me?"

I shrugged my shoulders a little. Maybe I was talking to her because I knew I could. I could talk to her because I was Elaine O'Dea, and I could decide to talk to anybody I wanted to whenever I wanted to talk to them. But I didn't say that out loud.

"In a few weeks we're going to be seniors," I told her. "I think maybe we're getting too old for this shit."

As soon as I said it, I realized I believed every word of what I'd just said.

Alice rolled her eyes and laughed a little, but not a funny ha-ha laugh. More like an I-can't-believe-you-would-say-that laugh. "Easy for you to say," she huffed.

She had a point, and I didn't say anything for a minute or so. I heard the tock of Misty's clock and the laughter between her and Ms. Cooper. I stared at the faded pink linoleum under my new strappy sandals.

We were going to be seniors. And maybe she had texted Brandon while he was driving, but that didn't mean that Brandon had to answer his phone. And maybe she did have sex with two guys in the same night, but hadn't Brandon probably had sex with five times that number of girls the summer before junior year alone? And maybe she had made out with him in the coat closet during the eighth grade dance when he and I were totally and completely *on again*, but hadn't Brandon been the one to choose to make out in the coat closet in the first place? And wasn't the eighth grade graduation dance pretty damn far away from senior year?

"Alice," I said, and I waited until she made eye contact with me again before I kept going, "look, if you want to start coming around my table at lunch again, you know, just to say hi, it might be a way to start smoothing things over. I mean, if you're interested."

She just stared at me, expressionless.

"I mean, I know you've been hanging out a lot with Kurt Morelli and everything," I said, although it occurred to me that I hadn't seen the two of them together much these past few weeks. "So maybe you're not even interested or whatever. But I'm just putting it out there."

Alice just kept looking at me. Not in a mad way, I don't think. But just sort of staring like she couldn't believe what she was hearing. I guess if I had been her I wouldn't have believed it either. I gave it one more shot. "Are you getting your hair done to go to the dance with Kurt?"

Alice gave me one of her big honking laughs that she was known for and that I hadn't heard all year, but it was cut with a tone that sounded super bitter. "No, I'm not going to the dance with Kurt Morelli or anyone else. And I don't hang around with him anymore, anyway," Alice said. "He's no different from anyone else in this town."

I was surprised by what she said, but I was also sure that Alice couldn't be more wrong. Kurt Morelli had been different from everyone in Healy since the day he'd moved here back in elementary school, and he'd been proving he was different ever since.

"Oh, sorry. I thought he was your friend."

"Well, I thought a lot of people were my friends," Alice said. It could have come out sounding a lot icier than it did, but the way Alice said it—like she was just flatly stating the facts we both knew were true—made her words feel like they were hanging right over me. I thought about the Slut Stall. Part of me wanted to tell her I'd only written in it that one time and everything, but I didn't think Alice would care if it had been one time or twenty.

"I'm sorry I brought up Kurt," I answered. "I thought you guys liked hanging out together, but I guess I was wrong. I know he's sort of freaky deaky or whatever, but you can't say he's anything like the rest of us. First off, he hung out with you when no one else would, and it honestly seemed like you guys were having a good time. Plus, he's, like, a crazy genius. He knows more than the teachers."

Alice just looked away, down at the floor. "Yeah, well. I guess I have a way of turning everything around me into shit. Maybe he was my friend. Maybe he wasn't. I don't know anymore. Whatever."

"Fine. I was just saying."

A few more moments of silence passed, but Alice broke it this time.

"Who are you going to the dance with?"

"Jacob Saunders," I said with a shrug. Jacob was a graduating senior and captain of the varsity basketball team, and if you want me to be honest he was about as exciting as a bag of hammers.

Just then Misty stuck her head out and told us she was so sorry she was running late and did we mind waiting just a few more seconds?

I rolled my eyes at Alice and she rolled her eyes back at me. Then Alice picked up her copy of *Teen Vogue* and started reading it again. I figured she was done talking, so I grabbed a magazine and we sat there reading in silence until Ms. Cooper left and Misty called for Alice to come on back.

Just before she disappeared behind the reception area, Alice turned around and said, "Have a good time at the dance."

"Thanks," I answered.

I felt pretty good about what I had said, and I hoped Alice was grateful I'd said it. After all, she had to have known that me being nice to her in the cafeteria would be a sign to everybody else that it was time to stop the mess that had been going on all year. She had to know I had that kind of power.

But the truth is, I knew there was a pretty good chance Alice would never come by my table on Monday or any other day. The truth is, I wouldn't blame Alice Franklin if she never talked to me or anyone else in this town again.

There are some things, like your eighth grade boyfriend kissing some other girl at a middle school dance, that are easy to forgive.

And there are some things that are just unforgivable.

Alice

IT'S A LONG WALK TO GET TO WHERE I'M
going, almost to the other side of town. I think it seems longer
than it really is since spring in Texas lasts about two weeks, so
essentially it's already summer, which means it's ridiculously
hot. We have a few weeks left of school and the heat is just all-
consuming. Every year it arrives and people act like they can't
believe it's already here again. Like maybe if they'd been good
all year long the 100-degree weather would somehow pass us by
just once.

But it shows up every year, whether we like it or not.

I guess that's one of the reasons I've chosen to make this walk
in the evening. The heat isn't so bad then, even if there are a few
mosquitoes around, and it's actually sort of peaceful to walk the
Healy streets at dusk. Maybe one of the two or three good

things about living in this crappy town is it's small enough that you can walk pretty much anywhere to get there.

Even if it is hot enough to melt tar.

Like just the other week, I'd walked to the Curl Up and Dye to get my hair cut.

On the way there I'd had to walk past the Pizza Hut and the Walmart and the elementary school, and just like I did whenever I had time alone to think, I thought about the rejection.

The rumors.

The unending crap on the walls of that bathroom stall that I couldn't stop reading even though I knew I should and that nobody ever bothered to clean because black Sharpie doesn't come off so easily. (And I should know because I tried.)

How much did it hurt?

It was like a million paper cuts on my heart.

Because it was slow and not all at once. It wasn't a complete flip-flop of everything overnight. It was more gradual than that.

Which was actually worse, to be honest with you. At first, it was so subtle I thought maybe I was imagining it.

"Oh, Alice, I'm sorry, I forgot to save you a seat."

"Oh, Alice, I never got that text. Something is weird with my phone."

"Oh, nothing, Alice. We're just laughing at a stupid joke."

Obviously, I wasn't imagining it.

But it had to be gradual. So people would get used to it. So it would become easy for them to treat me like shit. So my best friend since freshman year could justify dumping me and telling everyone I had an abortion. So they could have the Slut Stall and enjoy having it.

So there could be enough time for me to become subhuman in their eyes.

I really can't handle talking about this for too long because it just hurts too much, but I do want to say that there is one thing I've learned about people: they don't get that mean and nasty overnight. It's not human nature.

But if you give people enough time, eventually they'll do the most heartbreaking stuff in the world.

Now I'm taking another walk. Past Memorial Park where families have picnics on the weekends and sometimes kids from Healy High go to smoke pot. Past the lit-up Walgreens sign advertising toilet paper on special. Past the First Methodist Church of Healy and St. Helen's and Salem Lutheran and Calvary Baptist Church, whose church sign reads "YOU THINK IT'S HOT HERE?"

They post that message every May. It's as much like clockwork as the heat itself.

My legs ache, and the sweat is trickling down my neck. I'm grateful for my short hair. I turn into a neighborhood full of some of the oldest homes in Healy, rambling two-story houses with wraparound porches and big yards. They're old and hard to keep up, I think. It's not like it's the rich people neighborhood. Honestly, I don't think Healy actually has any people living here who are really rich because if you had a ton of money, why would you choose to live here? But if I had to pick my favorite neighborhood in this pathetic little town, this one would be it.

Probably not just because of the houses. But because of who lives here.

I've been to this house once before, and as I walk up the steps to the porch, I check the time on my phone. I have a minute or so to wait and as I wait, my heart marches to a tune of nervousness and anticipation.

Finally, I take a deep breath and knock. I've told myself I'll count to one hundred before walking away. By the time I make it to twelve the door swings open.

Standing there is Kurt Morelli.

"Hello, Alice," he says, and when he sees that I am smiling, he smiles, too.

Things I Noticed About Kurt Morelli
After He Started Tutoring Me

- We're just about the same height, but he couldn't look me in the eye for the first month that he tutored me. Because I made him so nervous.

- He gave off the vibe of liking me the entire time— from the moment I got that note in my locker, which, by the way, I almost didn't open because I thought it was going to be some rude, disgusting note complete

194

with a gross cartoon of me. (It happened a couple of times.) But I did read the note, and I knew he liked me, but I also knew that he wouldn't try anything. At least, I believed that initially. And anyway, I did need the help in math. Then that first night I thought maybe he assumed I was *so* slutty I *would* sleep with him in exchange for math help. After all, who else was lining up to sleep with Kurt Morelli? I still smile to myself when I think about his face when I accused him of that. He looked like he wanted to melt into a puddle under the kitchen table just hearing the words *sleep with me* come out of my mouth. And then when he told me he thought I just deserved someone to be nice to me, I knew that even if he did like me, he wasn't going to try anything. And he never did.

• He's ridiculously smart. Like, ridiculously. I don't understand probably 20 percent of the words he uses. One time I told him that, and he smiled and said that it came from reading too much. "Is there such a thing as reading too much?" I asked him. "No, I guess not," he said, and he blushed again. In addition to being ridiculously smart, he is also a ridiculous blusher.

• When he eats, he chews each bite exactly seven times. I don't think he's aware of this. I noticed it the night I bought us pizza and the day he had me over for grilled cheese sandwiches. It's a little weird, I'll grant you that. But it's also sort of reassuring.

- He is an incredible gift giver. I felt so stupid when I didn't know what a first edition was, but when he told me, it made the copy of *The Outsiders* even better than I thought it was when I first opened it. I keep it on my nightstand and when I'm having an especially crappy day, like when I think even the teachers are looking at me weird, I open it up and I read the note Johnny wrote to Ponyboy on his death bed. The one where he tells him to stay gold.

"Do you want to sit down?" he asks, and I nod. We take a seat on the porch swing.

"Are you home alone?" I ask him.

"My grandmother is at church," he says. "Wednesday night fellowship."

"Of course," I say with a grin.

"So . . ." Kurt says. "I got your note."

"The one I slipped into your locker?"

Kurt nods yes. "I was wondering where you got that clever idea." He grins at his own joke. I love it when Kurt is silly. When he is, it's like this perfect mix of doing something that seems totally out of character but is actually totally in character once you get to know him.

"So you read it?" I ask.

"Yes," Kurt says, and I wonder if he has also memorized the words I chose so carefully the night before. Here's what it said:

Dear Kurt. Dearest Kurt. My dear Kurt. I want you to know that none of what happened before matters. I want you to know it's okay you didn't tell me about Brandon sooner. I want to tell you that I'm sorry for anything I said that hurt you and that you were right. That it wasn't fair for me to react the way I did. Because you've been everything to me this year, Kurt. You've been my friend. And I want you to know that I don't want to be friends with anyone else but you. I think I just needed some time to come to terms with all of it. To think it all through. This isn't nearly as poetic or adequate as if you had written it, but what I'm trying to say is that all is forgotten and all is forgiven. Not that there was ever anything, really, to forgive you for. If anything, I need to ask your forgiveness. I'll come by tonight at 7:30 exactly and if you answer your door when I knock, I'll know it means you feel the

same way and we can be friends again. If
you don't answer the door, I'll never
bother you again. Thanks for everything.
Alice.

"Alice, I want to explain—" Kurt starts, but I cut him off.

"There's nothing to explain, Kurt," I tell him. "Honestly." I notice he has a scar on his knee. I've never noticed it before. I remind myself to ask him later where he got it. Suddenly, I have a million things I want to know about Kurt Morelli. "Kurt, I want you to know, I'm just so sorry for anything—"

"Alice, I read your note, remember?" Kurt says, interrupting me. I grin at him as he keeps talking. "I've missed spending time with you, Alice. Tremendously."

"I've missed you, too," I say. "And I've missed your vocabulary."

"Tremendously?" he says, smiling.

"Oh, yes, tremendously," I answer.

I've got this certain kind of feeling about Kurt Morelli. I think I first realized it existed when I sat down to write him that note. Or maybe I first realized it during those miserable few weeks when we weren't friends. Or maybe I recognized it when Elaine O'Dea and I talked that afternoon at the Curl Up and Dye. Maybe I don't know when exactly I started feeling it. Maybe it's sort of like the way the Healy heat comes on so steadily you don't realize it's there until one morning you wake up and it's 102 degrees at seven in the morning. It seems like it happened overnight, but when you look back, you realize it was building slowly all along.

I think that's the way it's been for me and Kurt.

I know Kurt won't, so I reach over and take his hand, and I like the way his fingers lace up with mine, like we've held hands a million times before. I'm surprised at how sure his grip is and at how fast my heart is pumping. We sit in the silence of the Healy evening, surrounded by the comforting chorus of cicadas.

"Thank you, Kurt, for being here," I tell him.

"Thank you, Alice, for the same thing," he says back, his voice almost a whisper.

And then Kurt looks at me with his big, sweet eyes and he smiles at me with his nice, warm grin.

It's the kind of grin you can trust. The kind of grin you want to keep on seeing. The kind of grin you wear on your face when you know you're going places in this life.

Because Kurt Morelli is going places.

Someday, so will I.

ACKNOWLEDGMENTS

Huge thanks to my amazing agent Sarah LaPolla for absolutely everything. That call on the beach changed my life, and it wouldn't have happened without your guidance, support, and willingness to cheerfully put up with my neurosis. I owe you so much. Thanks also to Nathan Bransford for taking a chance, Sonya Sones for telling me I could, and Liz Peterson for reading early drafts and providing valuable feedback. Many thanks to everyone at Roaring Brook Press, especially my editor Nancy Mercado who works with a wise and gentle hand. Thanks also to Katherine Jacobs for giving this book special attention during its final stages.

Much love to my mom, dad, brother Christopher, and sister Stephanie for calling me a writer long before anyone else did.

And to Kevin, who suffered through rejections and revisions alongside me and served as the world's best sounding board through many late-night talk times. Texas-sized love to you and Elliott forever.

THE TRUTH ABOUT ALICE

bonus materials . . .

GOFISH

JENNIFER MATHIEU

What did you want to be when you grew up?
When I was very young, I used to say architect because I liked the sound of the word. Honestly, that's why I chose it. But I was terrible at math—it would have been an awful profession for me. I knew I wanted to do something with writing from a very young age—from elementary school, really. I didn't know what, but I knew I would make my life from words somehow.

What was your favorite thing about school?
When I was little, my favorite part of school was library time. I had a wonderful elementary school librarian named Mrs. Long. We would go down to the library as a class and sit around her feet on a carpet, and she would read these books to us. Her voice was just magical. Sometimes, we girls would play with each other's hair while she read, and she would always say in this gentle way, "Girls, this isn't a hair salon." It was so cute. I just adored those moments sitting crisscross applesauce and listening to stories. As I got older, my favorite thing about school was being good at it. I was a very focused student. It was important for me to do well, and I actually enjoyed organizing my work, doing my homework, and pushing myself on projects and papers. What can I say? I was and am a total nerd.

What were your hobbies as a kid? What are your hobbies now?

Like Kelsie in *The Truth About Alice*, I loved making shoe-box dioramas. I had a dollhouse and I was heavily into making up stories with the characters and acting out different voices for the different dolls. I made little dioramas for the characters to explore: a restaurant, a store, a chapel, and so on. I was into it well into junior high. With a husband, son, full-time teaching job, and my writing, I have very little time left for hobbies. I mainly read! If social media counts as a hobby, I could definitely claim that one, too.

What was your first job, and what was your "worst" job?

I started babysitting around my neighborhood when I was eleven or twelve, but my first actual job where I received a paycheck with taxes taken out was working at the now-defunct Blockbuster video chain. I was fifteen or sixteen and I worked the register, shelved videos, and assisted customers. My worst job was probably the summer before my senior year of college. I worked for a small public relations firm and I had to type up press releases for a company that made chain saws. It was totally soul-sucking and horrible, and the people weren't very nice. I quit after a few weeks and got a job waiting tables at a pizza place and was much happier. I was supposed to have spent the summer getting a "resume-builder" of a job, but I learned an important lesson that summer, which is that it's never worth it to stick with a job that makes you completely miserable. Life is too short.

What book is on your nightstand now?

I just finished *Sway* by Kat Spears, and I absolutely loved it. It's about a teenage guy who is sort of the Godfather of his high school—he can hook you up with just about anything, legal or illegal. At first he's sort of emotionally closed off and you know something is hidden inside his heart, but you're not sure how you're going to find out what it is. It's a terrific read. Despite some of the serious subject matter, there were some parts where I laughed out loud. It's Kat Spears's debut, and I can't wait to see what she does next.

How did you celebrate publishing your first book?
I had a launch party at Blue Willow Bookshop, my favorite indie bookstore in Houston, and I had a party with friends after that. Because *The Truth About Alice* is set in Texas, I had cookies made in the shape of Texas. They were so yummy.

Where do you write your books?
I type them on my laptop at the dining room table in my house, and sometimes I work at a little coffee shop down the street from where I live.

What sparked your imagination for *The Truth About Alice*?
A few things. One, my lifelong interest in small towns. Two, I wanted to write a sort of *Spoon River Anthology* for high school, with lots of voices weaving together to tell one big story that only the reader knows in full. Third, an article I read in *Seventeen* magazine in the early nineties about a young woman in Minnesota who became the victim of some horrible graffiti in a bathroom stall and, when she complained to her principal, nothing was done. She ended up suing the school because they refused to help her or stop the harassment. All of those stories helped inspire *The Truth About Alice*.

Did you ever experience bullying growing up?

Of course I experienced a lot of mean girl drama that drove me to tears on occasion, but no, I never experienced the sort of chronic abuse that to me defines bullying. Unfortunately, I have to say I witnessed bullying. There was a girl I went to school with when I was around eleven or twelve who was horribly made fun of by many in the class the entire time she was there, for three years, and while I don't think I actively participated, I never tried to stop anything. It's one of my biggest regrets.

What advice would you give someone who is facing bullying?

I know it's advice that's heard over and over, but I would recommend that they keep telling the adults in their lives until someone listens and helps. One thing I would never tell a teenager is, "It gets better. Just hang in there. You won't even remember this when you're older." That's terrible advice. When you're sixteen, a year in your life feels like forever. And serious bullying can leave lifelong scars. Keep asking for help. And find an outlet—music, writing, art, running around the block—to release your anger or sadness.

What is your favorite word?

I love the word *mortified*. I think it's such a delicious word, and I use it as often as I can.

If you could live in any fictional world, what would it be?

I would love to visit an Edith Wharton novel, just for a week or two, to witness the world of the super privileged of her day— it would be terrific people watching! As for living somewhere permanently, I think I would love to be best friends with Anne Shirley and live next door to her in Avonlea.

Who is your favorite fictional character?

It's impossible to choose just one, but I would say Margaret Simon from Judy Blume's *Are You There God? It's Me, Margaret*; Johnny Cade from S. E. Hinton's *The Outsiders*; Ruby Oliver from E. Lockhart's Ruby Oliver books; Park Sheridan from Rainbow Rowell's *Eleanor & Park*; and Merricat and Constance from Shirley Jackson's *We Have Always Lived in the Castle*.

What was your favorite book when you were a kid? Do you have a favorite book now?

My favorite book of all time when I was growing up was *The Outsiders*. It was incredibly special to me, and that's why I chose to include it in *The Truth About Alice*. The characters were so real to me, it's like I thought I could drive to Oklahoma and meet them. I think if I met S. E. Hinton, I might cry. It was just such a beautiful story with such heartbreaking characters. To be honest, it still ranks as one of my favorite books. I keep a list on my author website with some favorite books of all time, including books I fell in love with as an adult. I actually read a lot of nonfiction in addition to fiction. I love Chuck Klosterman, who writes about pop culture in such an intelligent way. One of the best books that I've read as an adult is called *Random Family*. The writer, Adrian Nicole LeBlanc, spent ten years following teenagers in a very poor section of the Bronx during the 1980s and wrote about their lives. It's so compelling and it's all true. The crazy connection is that Adrian Nicole LeBlanc actually wrote the article in *Seventeen* that helped inspire *The Truth About Alice*! She's a terrific journalist.

If you could travel in time, where would you go and what would you do?
Well, I'm obsessed with the 1950s and early 1960s because of the clothes and furniture. So I would go back in time and purchase all the dresses and shoes and chairs and sofas I could carry in my time machine and take it all back to the present day with me. Today's dollars would go so far back then. But I wouldn't want to live back then because even though it was glamorous in many ways, the era was far too conservative for my liking.

What's the best advice you have ever received about writing?
I once heard a saying that there are only three rules to writing but the problem is that no one knows what they are. The truth is that every writer is different. I've heard some writers say they love to write in longhand. Other writers I know plot out every single scene before they start. But that advice would never work for me. I think the best advice I have ever received is to just write and find the way that works for you.

What would you do if you ever stopped writing?
Sleep more and watch too much bad television.

Do you have any strange or funny habits? Did you when you were a kid?
I used to eat paper as a kid. I remember my sixth-grade English teacher, Mrs. Mullery, would catch me, and she would remind me of all the inks and dyes in the paper and how bad

they were for me, and I would still tear little pieces off the corners of pages and eat them. Fortunately, I've retired that habit. I don't know that I have any strange or funny habits now, but if you ask my husband, I bet he could list a bunch.

What do you consider to be your greatest accomplishment?
Getting up every single day and trying to be a compassionate person.

What would your readers be most surprised to learn about you?
I was a cheerleader in high school. Sometimes that one even surprises me.

Rachel Walker is devoted to God.

She prays every day, attends Calvary Christian Church with her family, helps care for her five younger siblings, dresses modestly, and prepares herself to be a wife and mother who serves the Lord with joy. But Rachel is curious about the world her family has turned away from, and increasingly finds that neither the church nor her homeschool education has the answers she craves. Rachel has always found solace in her beliefs, but now she can't shake the feeling that her devotion might destroy her soul.

devoted

a novel

JENNIFER MATHIEU

Keep reading for a sneak peek!

1

James Fulton is sweating like a sinner in church.

Which, of course, is exactly what he is.

All of us—the older kids my age and the mothers and the fathers and even the little toddlers whose feet don't touch the floor yet—all of us congregants of Calvary Christian Church of Clayton watch wide-eyed and silent from our metal folding chairs as James shifts his weight from one barrel-thick leg to the other, his ruddy face covered in a slick coat of perspiration. He squeezes his hands together as he sways back and forth, and a little map of sweat starts to form on the front of his yellow polyester short-sleeved shirt. Pastor Garrett stands off to the side, clutching his enormous Bible and nodding along with everything James says.

"I'm here before you with a purified heart," James continues, looking at his feet. His white-blond hair is newly shorn, making his flushed face seem even more scarlet. "I know I need to live radically for the Lord again. And I'm asking you to help me walk with God again because I know the punishment for sin is separation from the Lord and eternity in hell." Exhaling shakily and squeezing his hands together again, he makes the briefest of eye contact with the congregation before gazing back down at his feet.

My four-year-old sister Sarah is sitting in my lap, and she turns her little head to look at me and whispers too loudly, "Rachel, what'd that boy do?"

People shift in their seats around us at her question, but nobody says anything. "Shh, Sarah," I whisper back. "He's talking about how much he loves Jesus."

What James Fulton did was gratify the desires of the flesh, but I can't say that to Sarah. And I can't tell her that he looked at pictures of naked women on a computer and he got caught, and I can't tell her that he just got back from two weeks at Journey of Faith, a camp in east Texas where he spent hours in prayer and physical labor and repentance. Sarah's too little to understand about Journey of Faith.

She won't be too little to understand for much longer, of course. But for now, at least, it doesn't take much to distract her.

It seems one or two of us are sent to Journey of Faith every few years. By us I mean the older kids at Calvary Christian. Some are as young as thirteen or fourteen when they're sent away, and they always leave suddenly, spirited off by Pastor Garrett or a church elder, leaving the rest of us to consider the rumors we've heard about what Journey of Faith is all about. Long, forced hikes; little sleep; and endless, backbreaking physical work, along with hours spent alone studying Scripture. Those of us who've never gone put the pieces together from testimonies like the one James is delivering now. We know that Journey of Faith is a place where life is hard, but the Lord is supposed to work on your heart and transform you.

Everyone comes back looking like James.

His cheeks are cherry red, and the shame he carries radiates off him. He hasn't come out and explicitly stated his sin, but he knows we must know about how he's strayed. He knows we know about his stumbling block. We've learned about the sins that send some of us to Journey of Faith in the same way we've learned about the camp itself. In whispers and bits of whispers. In requests for prayers during youth fellowship and at evening Bible studies.

In the Scripture used by those who've fallen upon their return to the flock.

"So in closing," James continues, "I want to say that the Lord is leading me to share with you this verse from Psalms, a verse that the pastor at Journey of Faith shared with me in one of our sweet fellowships." I can tell he has practiced this part many times from the way his voice picks up speed and volume. "'Wherewithal shall a young man cleanse his way? By taking heed thereto, according to thy word. With my whole heart have I sought thee: O let me not wander from thy commandments.'" There's a ripple of nodding heads, and at last James makes his way back to his row to join his parents. His mother squeezes him around his broad, beefy shoulders and his father nods approvingly, and I see how James smiles at them, a quick upturned smile that disappears as quickly as it arrives.

Pastor Garrett makes a commanding motion toward the corner where Mrs. Carter sits at the upright piano, and as I hear the opening notes of "It's Through the Blood," I lift my little sister in my arms and stand up to get ready to sing.

⚬⚬⚬

After the service ends, all of us spill out onto the weedy patch of grass and gravel in front of the church. I put Sarah down and watch her speed off and start racing around with some of the countless other small kids her age.

I weave through the crowd, smiling back brightly at everyone who smiles at me as I try to keep watch on my younger siblings. When I was little like them I could climb back into the family van after services with my worn-out copy of *Anne of Green Gables*, but the last time I tried that, Dad said I wasn't showing a sweet spirit. I'm seventeen now, and not only am I supposed to watch out for my little brothers and sisters, I'm supposed to be their model of proper behavior.

"Rachel! Rachel!" Someone is yelling my name from across the parking lot. I turn and spot my older sister, Faith, waving me over with the one arm she isn't using to hold her infant son, Caleb. It's early May in Texas and five hundred billion degrees, but somehow Faith isn't sweating, and her lavender blouse and knee-length denim skirt don't have a spot of baby puke on them.

"Hi," I say, joining her and some of the other young mothers of the congregation, several just a few years older than me. They stand in a loose circle holding their little ones, and their carefully groomed appearances and enthusiastic smiles make me run my fingers through my long, dark curls so I don't look too disheveled. I wish not for the first time that my hair were straighter like Faith's, but almost immediately I hear my father's voice reminding me that *a sound heart* is *the life of the flesh: but envy the rottenness of the bones.* I imagine my bones strong and pure, constructed of nothing but molecules of good thoughts, absent of any vanity. I smile at everyone and wiggle my fingers at my little nephew Caleb, choosing to give him my full attention while the other girls chatter around me.

"I was just saying," Faith starts, shifting Caleb from one hip to another with ease, "that James's testimony really moved me, really moved us all, actually, and I think the Lord has laid it on our hearts to try and organize some time for fellowship, where some of us older girls get together with some of the younger girls and talk about, you know, modest dress. About helping the boys and the young men in their struggle to remain spiritually pure. Just, you know, recommitting to that idea of biblical femininity."

Faith's voice is filled with enthusiasm, each sentence practically spilling on top of the next one. The other girls are nodding. Faith has always been good at helping us think of others. When we were little, she taught me to flip over magazine covers in the grocery checkout line if they had immodest images of girls and women that might tempt the eyes of our brothers.

"That sounds like it would be nice," I say. Faith is talking on excitedly when my eyes spot James Fulton by the side of Calvary Christian. He's alone. The quick smile he shared with his parents at the end of the service is gone now, and he leans against the church wall, staring out at a cinder-block building in the lot next door. The building used to house a tractor-and-lawn-mower repair service, but it was abandoned a long time ago, and now it's just a crumbling mess of a place. It's not anything to look at, that's for sure, but James is watching it like it's something worth watching.

His cheeks still appear red—maybe this time from the heat outside—and he takes a big gulp of air and tips his head back against the side of the church, shifting his gaze to the blue, cloudless sky. I imagine myself stepping up in front of the entire congregation to admit my deepest sins, and I know that James feels an embarrassment so painful he can barely stand to look any of us in the eye.

We should show compassion toward sinners, and James looks so pitiful standing there all by himself that I want somebody to walk over to talk to him about the weather or where he got his yellow polyester shirt or something that doesn't have to do with his sinful behavior or Journey of Faith or how proud we are of how he's walking with Jesus. But nobody goes to him, least of all me.

"I mean, I think we would be really honoring James's testimony if we put his words into action, don't you think?" Faith continues, almost breathless in her excitement.

"Oh, definitely," I answer, offering a quick smile.

When my father finds me a few minutes later and tells me it's time to leave, James Fulton is still standing there alone.